LIGHTER THAN AIR

Letters From the Past Series

TINA CLOUGH

LIGHTER THAN AIR

Copyright © Tina Clough 2023

The author asserts her moral right to be identified as the author of this work.

PAPERBACK ISBN 978-1-99-118714-7

All rights reserved. No part of this book may be reproduced, stored in a retrieval system, or transmitted in any form or by any electronic or mechanical means including photocopying, recording, information or retrieval systems, or otherwise, without prior permission in writing from the publisher, with the exception of book reviewers, who may quote short excerpts in reviews.

Lightpool Publishing

www.lightpoolpublishing.com

Cover and book design by Andrene Low

Chapter 1

Very early in the morning, the office sometimes felt like a different country, a territory of calm potential, untainted by personalities and outside influences. After disarming the alarm system Sofia remained just inside the door for a few moments and listened to the silence, really heard the silence, not just absence of sound but a concrete entity as substantial as a physical object. I love it when it's silent like this, early in the morning, she thought, and walked slowly past the reception desk and along the passage to her room. Nobody would talk to her, and her train of thought would be uninterrupted, leading to clear conclusions.

She hung her new orange jacket behind the door and sat down at her desk. The early sun cast a bright wedge of light on the wall opposite and just reached the corner of the painting she bought in a flea market in France a few years ago. A landscape that reminds her of a beach in Normandy, the beach where her father drowned. My earliest memory, she thought, and I didn't invent it. The first time her mother saw the painting, well, the only time, she said, 'Oh, my God, how on earth did you find that?''

Over the years Sofia had realised that her mother did not believe that she really did remember that day, but her memories are full of vivid details, things she could not possibly have invented after the event.

It was ten past six on a November Thursday and she had woken very early and instantly known that getting into the office at least an hour and a half before everyone else was the perfect thing to do. Her week was going to be very busy and as always, she was determined to be well prepared with nothing left to the last minute. She had an upcoming fraud trial that could go either way, a tricky thing with only one witness and many assumptions, but as clear as glass in Sofia's mind. She could nearly smell it, the half-hidden trail of deception and legal-seeming trickery that had taken a man's entire life savings and left him broken. Modern fraudsters, she thought as she sat down and pulled the case folder towards her, for every one of them there is at least one gullible victim they can take to the cleaners, however clearly others can see in retrospect that the promised return on investment could not possibly be real. And as usual, the problem was getting the money back. In this case the fraudster claimed to have gambled the money away, and it was true that the money had disappeared out of his bank account over a long period of time, but there was something about the sums he had repeatedly withdrawn that made Sofia suspicious.

Tapping her front teeth with her pen, she wondered what more she could do or find out, one more witness or one more fact, but she could think of nothing constructive. For some reason this case had taken on a level of importance in her mind she could not explain even to herself. It was a test of her abilities, the urge to bring justice to her elderly client and to return his savings to him, but also driven by her acute dislike of the fraudster. She had seen him once, heard his voice and felt an overwhelming need to punish him. The look of smug self-confidence and his casual stance had riled her, and now it was not enough for him to be punished for fraud, he must lose that money, wherever and however he had concealed it. The story of having lost it by gambling held no credibility for her.

. . .

An hour and a half later she sat absorbed in her notes for another trial fast approaching, adding the occasional detail and considering how best to present what evidence she had. Various noises from other parts of the office had gradually filtered into her mind, but when her phone let out a violent blast of trumpet music, she nearly jumped out of her skin. Frantic to silence it she scrabbled through the papers on her desk, grabbed the phone and pressed the green button without checking who the call was from.

'You won!' said the overly loud voice of her friend, Marcus, and she realised that the phone was on speaker and put it down on the desk. 'Hands down - the vote's in, and you've blasted everyone else out of water. Where the hell did you get a phrase like that from anyway?'

'What do you mean "where did a get it from"?' She laughed. 'The competition rules say the quote must come from a book or a document - and it did. And what are you doing awake at this hour, it must be about five in the morning at your end?'

'Couldn't sleep, so I got up to see what's going on in the world. A couple of people have suggested you made that phrase up, it's too ridiculous to be true, so now they want to know the name of the book you found it in.'

She could sense his malicious glee; he was hoping she had no proof. He'd never forgiven her for pointing out last time, that she had won the competition more times than anyone else. Marcus's intense competitive streak made him an irresistible target for teasing when he didn't win.

'Don't be silly – it's from a romantic historical novel I read a while ago. I'll find it on my Kindle and post the title tonight. Very entertaining. You're just jealous you didn't win – again.'

He laughed and that made Sofia laugh too, the way his laugh always had, irresistibly contagious. And as always, when he laughed the image of him popped into her mind, tall and gangly and a bit uncoordinated in a way that seemed to affect his clothing as well as his movements. Did anyone else ever turn up so often with his shirt coming untucked and his shoelaces threatening to unravel?

'OK, mind you do that. I can't wait to see the reactions when the others find out you read romantic novels. I mean, who would have thought? The most serious one of us, no time for frivolities and now she reads historical romances?'

'Oh, shut up, Marcus! All women read them, it's just that we never tell any men – and mostly no other women either. It's a flight from reality, light relief.' She smiled at her secretary who was standing in the open door with a folder in her hand and an incredulous look on her face. 'But it was such a great phrase – I really like it, I kind of pictured it happening and it made me laugh.'

She ended the call and turned to Clare, who came in and put the folder on her desk. 'Here's the affirmation from Mrs Horton re that affidavit, just in time. Talk about leaving it to the last minute. Do you want me to get you a coffee?'

Sofia smiled and wondered how much of that conversation Clare had heard.

'I'd love a coffee, thanks, And I'd be very grateful if you could take my phone and get rid of that ring tone – the call was from my contact listed as Marcus, so it's probably specific to him. I let Bitsy play a game on my phone when she came for a visit yesterday, and she must have changed something. She's just learning how to do all kinds of tricky things.'

'I'm sorry to make your day worse, but you *must* call your mother – as soon as you can,' said Clare looking slightly uncomfortable. 'She called three times yesterday when you didn't want to be disturbed, and she's already called again this morning, and the meeting excuse is wearing thin. Now she's abusing *me* because you've blocked her on your phone – she doesn't know she's been blocked - she thinks you always turn your phone off in meetings, but I'm afraid I'll lose my temper with her soon.'

Knowing how vicious her mother could be to helpless frontline staff when thwarted, Sofia instantly felt guilty for having left Clare to make excuses rather than take her mother's calls herself for a couple of days. Talking to her mother was often irritating and occasionally infuriating, so the longer it could be put off the better, particularly when she was busy.

'God, I'm so sorry – I shouldn't have left you to fend her off for so long! Of course, I'll call her back. I'll call her from the landline, so she can't see that my cell phone number comes up as "unknown".'

'You could always explain it away as something Bitsy did.' Clare laughed and took the phone, but in the doorway she turned. 'Romantic novels? Really? And a ridiculous phrase competition?'

Sofia knew that the only way to prevent this becoming an obsession, which intriguing things sometimes did with Clare, to be constantly revisited and speculated about, knew the quickest way to put this to bed was to tell her.

'A competition a group of us stated in law school – about terrible phrases we found in legal acts and documents. And then if morphed into phrases from films and books, which extended the scope by miles. We run it in a closed Facebook group because we're scattered over the globe now – every month we vote for a winner.'

'And?'

'Oh, the phrase.' It made Sofia grin even thinking about it. 'I think it's great, listen to this – "his voice trickled down her spine like warm honey". What do you think about that?'

Clare burst out laughing and put her hands up in surrender. 'Of course, that won! Did you really find it in a book?'

'Oh, yes – a so-called historical romance I read a few months ago on my Kindle, light relief, you know. And I've got that kind of tiresome memory that stores random nonsense and annoys everyone else, so I remembered it verbatim.'

Chapter 2

As soon as Clare left her room, Sofia dialled her mother's cell phone and composed herself to sound calm, to not rise to baits or criticisms and not sound as if she couldn't wait to end the call.

Instead of a normal response to her, "Hi mum, how's the tour going?", her mother burst out in an aggravated tone of voice, 'You are *impossible*! I'm wasting half my life trying to get to talk to you and I'm sure that secretary of yours is lying through her teeth, I bet you weren't in a meeting at all, you're just trying to avoid talking to me! I don't know what I have done to deserve an only child who ignores and disrespect me, it's a tragedy.'

Sofia clenched her teeth, counted to ten and said, 'But how are you, mum? Is the tour going well?'

Sometimes refusing to reply to her tirades and

offering no explanations or excuses was the quickest way out, and today it worked.

'Oh, the tour is going *great*! I'm doing interviews at nearly every stop and most places are sold out – the Barber is very popular in Australia – well, it's popular everywhere, I suppose. And now there's talk of a TV interview too, a nationwide station – perhaps they'll use a clip from the performance, that's always such a thrill. And the Brisbane season has been extended by two days, so now we only have one free day before Cairns. But I'm calling about granddad – when you saw him last, was he worse?'

Sofia thinks back to her last, no more than normally confusing visit to her grandfather when she drove to Masterton for the day to visit him

'I don't think he was any worse than usual – it was a couple of weekends ago, and I took him out for lunch which he enjoyed. He got a bit confused about what he'd ordered and claimed he'd ordered something else, and then he thought he was taking me out, but we got around that. And you'll be relieved to hear I didn't let him drive, as he thought he would do. So, pretty normal for him. Why? Has something happened?'

'The care home called me yesterday and said he's frantic, he says he must talk to you as soon as possible – not just talk on the phone, you must go and see him. Something about a letter he wants you to help him with and it has to be you. I don't know why they don't have your phone number. The nurse who called said he's very agitated about it and he didn't sleep at all the night before – he kept wandering around the place and going into other people's rooms and causing all sorts of trouble. You should go tomorrow!'

Really, thought Sofia, does she think I can just drop everything and drive to Masterton on a weekday? She wouldn't do it in my place, even if she wasn't in Australia. And why didn't they call me directly, I thought they had my phone number.

'I can't tomorrow, but I'll go on Saturday, it's just one day away.'

Her mother's voice rose and took on the shrill note that meant either trouble or tears coming up. 'You have to, Sofia – he's asked for you specifically and he's the only grandparent you've got left. He could be dead by Saturday - we don't know what might happen with someone his age getting agitated!'

After an exhausting exchange she ended the call and Clare walked into a silent room with Sofia making notes again and frowning in concentration.

'All sorted – the phone I mean. Bitsy had changed to call alert for three or four people to specific ones, I checked the lot – all very loud and boisterous. I only left the signal you set up for your mother – in case you unblock her at some stage. How is Bitsy getting on with her reading?'

'She's doing really well - I'm so proud of her! We've moved on to those early chapter books now – you know, big print, short sentences and lots of pictures. She reads them to me, and then as a reward I either read to her or I let her have a treat, usually playing a game on my phone.'

'Isn't she lucky to have you next door? Who else would take the trouble to help her?'

'Probably nobody until it's too late. Her parents aren't very patient – they're such a nice couple but I don't think they understand that her problems with reading could affect the rest of her life, not just education but jobs too.'

'What do the parents do? I don't think you've ever told me.'

'That's the trouble - they do so much that they hardly have time for Bitsy. They both work full time, he's studying online for an accounting degree and Billie, that's the mum, is addicted to the gym.' Sofia smiled. 'Not that I mind, I love her visits and it's nice that I can do something worthwhile for her. She's very entertaining too – tells me how I should do my hair and what kind of shoes I should wear.'

'Do you have a photo of her?' asked Clare, who

was more than twenty years older than Sofia and had two grandchildren, whose photos were often bought out in the lunchroom.

'Here - have a look.'

Clare took the phone and said, 'Oh, I didn't realise she's Chinese. She's very cute!'

'Immigrants from Hong Kong, but they've been here for years, Bitsy was born here.'

Coming home late, tired after a long day, Sofia put a frozen Thai dinner in the microwave oven, poured a glass of wine and sat down to reschedule her plans for Saturday when she was supposed to go to the Italian food festival at the Westpac stadium with Sian and Barton, and which she would now miss.

'Duty calls,' she said to Barton. 'Aged grandfathers with dementia wait for no one, so I'll have to miss it, which is a bugger because I missed it last time too.'

Shrieks erupted in the background and Barton said quickly, 'Hang on, I have to go and see who's been murdered this time – Sian is out shopping.'

Sofia leaned her shoulder against the fridge and watched her dinner going around in the microwave oven, thinking of the Somerville fraud case and wondering if her key witness was going to hold it together or start floundering. Witnesses, she thought, often unpredictable and in this case, more so than usual. Mr Somerville's such a talker, he gets distracted and veers off in unexpected directions, very hard to keep on topic.

And then Barton was back, chuckling. 'No, we still have three — the boys beheaded one of Anneliese's dolls. But don't worry about Saturday, we can go on Sunday. Probably better anyway because Sian's parents are taking the children out to lunch and a movie then, so we won't have to chase them all over the place.'

Chapter 3

The drive over the Remutaka Hill was surprisingly smooth despite it being Saturday, and Sofia pulled in at the summit lookout where she often stopped to enjoy the panoramic views.

A middle-aged couple were the only others there, and after a couple of minutes the woman walked over to Sofia. 'Excuse me, are you a local?' she asked. 'Oh, good. We're here on a holiday from England and we're fascinated with a little bird over there, very friendly and comes right up to us. You might know what it is.'

'Oh, that's a fantail – piwakawaka in Maori,' said Sofia when she got close. 'They often hang around people – we stir up little insects as we move around, and they catch them in flight. Sometimes if you're walking through the bush, they follow you for ages and flit around your head. Mostly they're very friendly and not at all scared of people.'

'Pity it's so fast,' said the man, who was holding his phone. 'I just can't get a photo of it – or perhaps I'm just too slow. I've taken half a dozen shots and all they show is the view – not the bird.'

'They *are* tricky,' said Sofia, who had experienced the same problem in the past, before she discovered how burst mode worked on her phone. 'If you want me to, I can try.'

With the couple in their original spot next to the manuka trees at the edge of the drop-off, Sofia retreated a couple of steps with the man's phone and waited. After a moment the fantail appeared again, flitting around the couple as if it was playing a game. She used burst mode three times and then checked what she had captured.

'Here you are.' She handed the phone back and watched the couple scrolled through the images.

'Wow!' said the wife. 'How did you take so many shots in such a short time? They're fabulous!'

'It's called burst mode - the camera takes several shots per second as long as you continue to hold the button down, or that's how it works on my phone and on this one too. I only discovered it recently myself, but it's very useful.'

'I had no idea you could do this, thank you very

much,' said the husband and gave his wife a little push with his elbow. 'You might have been right – I *should* read the manual when I buy a new phone.' He turned to Sofia. 'She's usually right about things like that, but I hate reading manuals.'

'Don't we all?' said Sofia, who always read the manual before she used anything new. The couple, whose names she never discovered, were keen to tell her where they had been so far and where they were going, and she in turn told them that she was going to visit her grandfather who was in a dementia unit.

'What a shame,' said the woman. 'My dad got dementia and then he got Capgras syndrome, so he thought I was an impostor when I visited and asked the staff to call the police! Happened every few times I went, and it drove me crazy, I never knew what to expect.'

'Something to look forward to,' said Sofia and smiled. 'So far he remembers who I am, but he is getting progressively worse, though I must say his confusion is sometimes very entertaining. Last time I took him out for lunch, and he started a flirtation with a waitress who was at least sixty-five years younger than he is and made her quite embarrassed – I think he forgot he's a very old man now.'

. . .

When Sofia parked in the visitors' carpark, she sat for a moment studying the resthome, which looked rather like a hotel with an imposing facade and immaculate gardens. Every time she came, she was struck by how much money had been spent on the landscaping and the impressive entrance, presumably intended to make families feel comfortable about leaving an aging relative there, as if the care inside must match the exterior.

The reception desk was empty, but she heard raised voices in the distance, then a shriek of pain. She headed down the long hallway with handrails on both sides, but otherwise also very like a hotel, if you discounted the elderly residents standing in their doorways, looking in the direction of the noise.

Where the second wing branched off the hallway, she found a pair of elderly men wresting on the floor and shouting abuse at each other with a caregiver and a nurse trying to pull them apart. A walking-fame lay on its side on the far side of the wrestlers, and the nurse had a firm grip on the topmost fighter, who was holding on to the other man's beard with both hands. The caregiver turned to Sofia and said, 'If I can get around them to the other side, perhaps we can get his hands off the beard.'

The male nurse looked up and said, 'Yes, do that, please – I'm not making any progress from this angle.' But instead, Sofia knelt down on the floor and looked sideways up at the face of the topmost wrestler and said firmly, 'Let go of that man's beard *right now*, granddad, or I will go straight home again!'

He looked at her, and she could see the exact second when he recognised her, then suddenly he let go of the other man's beard and the nurse raised him to his feet.

'Sofia!' said her grandfather. 'Darling – thank God you've come! You've got to help me, this man's stolen my letter and he won't give it back.'

The caregiver lifted the walking frame, raised the bearded man to his feet and escorted him to his room, and the nurse turned to Sofia. 'I think I should say "thank God you've come" too. Your grandfather's been on a mission for a couple of days now to find a letter he's lost, and he thinks someone's hiding it.'

He turned to Sofia's grandfather and said firmly, 'We can't have you going into other people's rooms and start looking through their drawers, Angus, you know that. It's no wonder Bertrand got so angry. But now Sofia's here, she'll help you find it.'

'Let's hope so,' said Sofia, 'but I've no idea what this letter is – or if it even exists.'

Chapter 4

Sofia led her grandfather to his room and closed the door around them. 'What is this all about, granddad? What's this letter you're searching for?'

'You know, the letter I wrote for you,' he said impatiently and tapped his fingers on his thigh the way he always did when he was irritated or impatient. 'The letter you've got to keep until I die. I told you about it when you came last time but I think I forgot to give it to you.'

She knew that telling him he had never said anything about a letter would get her nowhere, so instead she tried another tactic that had worked in the past. "Remind me, grandad – I think I've forgotten what you said.'

'Are you're getting forgetful?' He laughed, a

suddenly switch in mood that was becoming familiar. 'You know, the letter with my confession.'

'Ah yes, now I remember,' said Sofia mendaciously, hoping that having at least one clue about the missing letter would lead her somewhere, though confession seemed an odd word in the context. 'And now it's missing?'

'I put it somewhere – somewhere safe. I mean, I wouldn't want anyone else to read it – not until I'm dead. I recall saying that to you, not until I'm dead, I said, it's for you to keep for me until then. It's somewhere here.' He made a sweeping gesture around the room. 'And then I went to look for it and it wasn't there.'

'And you've looked everywhere? Searched the whole room?' She knew this was unlikely, but she needed to find something that would trigger a memory in that haphazard mind of his. 'All you drawers? Amongst your books?'

'I've looked everywhere – so someone must have stolen it, a lot of things go missing here, the place is full of thieves. It's not the first time things have disappeared, you know. They took my wallet once and then they put in my sock drawer when I made a fuss about it.' He shook his head. 'I suppose they got worried they'd be found out.'

Sofia knew better than to get into any kind of

discussion about the missing, and then surprisingly found, wallet, a recurring theme for some time. 'Would you mind if I look around for the letter?'

'All right,' he said, disgruntled and frustrated. 'You can look as much as you like, but you won't find it – I've already looked everywhere.'

For the next hour Sofia meticulously worked her way around her grandfather's room; his wardrobe, checking pockets and inside shoes, the cabinet and drawers in his bathroom, under and between everything in his chest of drawers and the cluttered table beside his armchair. She took all his magazine from the rack on the other side of the armchair and flipped the pages before she moved on to his bookcase and turned every book upside down and shook it. And then finally, in his bedside table, there it was, acting as a drawer liner, a large brown envelope and on the side facing down, *Important* written with in pencil and *for Sofia* in ballpoint pen.

'Is this it?' she asked her grandfather and held it up. 'It was in the drawer of your bedside table, under all the bits and pieces. No wonder you didn't notice it.'

'Ah, yes – that's where I put it, I remember now. I should have told you,' said her grandfather calmly. He had just returned from lunch in the dining room and seemed unsurprised by her find. Looking hard at the envelope Sofia was holding, as if there was a possibility it was the wrong one, he added, 'Yes, yes, that's the right one - good girl! You take it now and keep it until I die and then you can open it.'

Knowing how randomly her grandfather could change his mind, often from one moment to the next, Sofia folded the thick envelope with some difficulty and stuffed it deep into her bag, where he wouldn't see it and then change his mind and say he wanted to keep it after all. Avoiding a repeat of this saga of suspicion and paranoia was her top concern, so instead of asking any questions she said, 'Granddad – how about I write a note for you, so you don't forget that we've found the letter? Just a reminder – so you know for sure it's safe now.'

'I suppose so – but I won't forget. You know that I don't often forget things.' The look he gave her was one of tolerant patience, the way a parent looks at a child who insists on something unnecessary.

'I'll just go down to the dining room and ask them to bring us cup of coffee each and a biscuit to celebrate, and I'll get a note done for you at the same time.'

She knew the nurses would have a computer she could use, but on her way through the foyer, Sofia saw a woman at a desk in the administrator's office, so she knocked on the half open door and pushed it a bit wider. 'Hi, I didn't realise you'd be here in the weekend. I'm sorry to disturb you, but would you have time to help me for a few minutes? I'm trying to avoid my grandfather causing another uproar about that lost letter.'

Fifteen minutes later she was sitting in her grandfather's room with a cup of coffee after putting a laminated sign on the wall beside the door, while he continued watching a rugby match on his TV.

'I've got to leave now grandad, but I've put that sign for you there,' she said after a while and pointed. 'Just in case. I don't want you to worry about the letter again now that we've found it. I'll take the cups back to the kitchen.'

He looked at her as if she was talking nonsense, half impatient, half pitying. 'Don't worry, I won't forget - but thank you, darling.' His attention went straight back to the TV when she kissed him, and she left with an internal sigh of relief.

As she walked to her car Sofia wondered how long it would be before that sign disappeared off the wall, and she pictured in her mind how the caregivers would find the replacement sign in the office, already printed and laminated with a Velcro dot on the back, ready to be put up instead, until the first sign was located again.

How the staff here have the patience to deal with

their charges, I'll never know, she thought, I simply couldn't do it, endless confusion and frustration, interlaced with random fury and even violence. Should I tell mum that he was in a real fight with that other poor man? Probably best not to, God knows how she would take it. I've never seen him like that before, but I had heard about dementia making people violent - it was so strange to see him fighting like that, he's always been such a calm and mild-mannered man.

Driving south through Wairarapa, then over the Remutaka road with the slanting late afternoon sun dramatically emphasising the folds of the ravines and valleys, she carried on an internal debate about how to proceed. If she told her mother that she now had the much talked about letter in her possession, the most likely outcome would be that Patsy's temperamental, opera diva persona would take over. Patsy Sylvester was probably nearly as famous for her temper and her public tantrums as she was for her admittedly gorgeous mezzo voice, thought Sofia, and she was hard to deal with when she was in full flight. Odds were that she would insist on opening the envelope right away to find out what was inside it, whatever Sofia said. Could she risk lying about it, saying her grandfather had made her write on the outside what his instructions were? That might restrain Patsy, but there was no guarantee it would. And then just as she reached the summit of the Remutaka hill she hit on the solution and laughed to herself, turned on her current favourite music and relaxed.

As soon as she got home and after thinking deeply about what to say, Sofia unblocked her mother on her phone and sent her a carefully crafted text message, hoping to orchestrate a time for a phone call that suited herself: "Call me when you can tomorrow. I'm going out for early drinks now and then dinner so muting my phone - and going out again to a food festival about 11 am tomorrow. The letter has been found and I have it. S xx"

Chapter 5

Later that evening with the last daylight nearly gone, when Sofia pulled down the blinds and reached for the little switch beside the balcony door, she once again reflected how lucky she was to have bought the apartment from an interior designer. When she first moved in, she had paid no attention to the switch, but one winter evening a couple of months later, she idly flicked it and stood back fascinated. Behind the dark apricot-coloured Roman blinds lights had come on, and the soft glow was enough to light the room indirectly, the way the last sunset light might on a clear night. She had raised one blind to investigate and found little LED strips mounted at the head of the window-fames, where the blinds hid them even when pulled up, like a little piece of magic.

Going to the kitchen to put her frozen shepherd's pie in the microwave oven, she poured a glass of wine and pulled the folded brown envelope out of her bag that she had left on a chair by the dining table. The envelope slid out of her fingers and fell to the floor scattering the contents in under the table. When she got down on her knees and scrambled around under the table, she was surprised by the number of small pieces of paper that had floated away in different directions. With her hands full she got to her feet and dumped the untidy pile on the table; two large sheets of paper, a handful of smaller papers and one newspaper cutting. The envelope was intact and had simply opened, as if the glue on the flap had dried up and become useless. I can Sellotape it up, she thought, and it will look as if it's always been that way, no harm done, and then her eyes fastened on the newspaper cutting and she sat down to look at it properly.

The yellowed cutting was part of a column of minor local news from some provincial paper with one short paragraph circled in pencil: *The vagrant who has sat on the pavement outside the South End fish and chips shop the last couple of weeks seems to have moved on, but his bundles and his coat were still on the pavement this morning, Mr Arnott, who owns the shop, told our reporter. "Not that I minded him being there", he added, "but a lot of women didn't like it, though I don't think he ever did anything wrong. I've put his belongings in the shed behind the shop so if he comes back, he can have them. We have heard he came here from Manawatu, but we don't know if that is correct, and someone said his name is Bill."*

There was a date pencilled in the top righthand corner, 23 May 1962, and she thought idly that it was about two months after her mother was born. I wonder why he kept it? she thought and moved the cutting to one side. I might as well look at this stuff, not that I was planning to open the envelope, but here it all is, right in front of me and now I'm intrigued.

The next sheet of paper was A4 size and handwritten on both sides, clear and tiny writing with the lines very close together, done with a pencil. She took the glass of wine and sat down in her armchair, turned the standard light on and put the bundle of loose papers on her lap. Five minutes later, having read both sides of the handwritten sheets of paper twice, she stared without focus at the opposite wall and tried to process the implications of what she had just read. After a couple of minutes, she got up, fetched a legal pad and a pen and made a few notes, just as she would when reading evidence and preparing for a court case. The ping from the oven had gone unnoticed; she was deeply engrossed in a family mystery that seemed nearly unbelievable.

Thinking back to the phone conversation with her mother the previous day, she was grateful that she then had no idea about the contents of the envelope or sounding casual and natural would have been very hard. Spreading the pieces of paper out on the dining table she tried to sort them into some kind of order. Seven of the small notes were written by her grandfather, the other four by her grandmother. Only the newspaper cutting and the two A4 sized sheets were dated, the smaller notes were not only undated, but most were also unsigned.

Fourteen pieces of paper, she thought, most of them probably torn from a little ruled notepad, the kind you make shopping lists on, and they have changed my life; not only my perception of my grandparents, but my ideas of right and wrong. Is doing wrong ethically OK if it saves suffering for another person and provided it harms nobody else?

Sofia had no sooner sat down with her re-heated dinner, still wondering what she should do about the confession letter as she now thought of it, than her phone buzzed. She glanced at the screen, saw it was from her cousin Storm and decided to take it even if her dinner got cold again in the process.

'I'm coming to Wellington to celebrate mum's

sixty-fifth – she's insists it's a landmark birthday,' he said and chuckled. 'Do you want to join us for dinner at Logan Brown? It's on Thursday next week. Sorry about the short notice, but we only just decided on this.'

'I'd love to! Why is it here? She hasn't moved, has she?'

'No, Fliss will never leave, she's still in Golden Bay amongst her crowd of aging hippies, but Summer and I are giving her a week in a really good hotel in Wellington as a birthday present, so she can check out museums and art galleries. She's been a couple of times to see grandad, but she's never taken the time to do a lot. Summer's coming up for four days, so I thought we could make it a family reunion kind of thing, and all go to see grandad too. I know Thursday is a weird day to have it, but it's the actual birthday.'

'I feel terrible that I haven't kept track of it – I knew her pensioner birthday was two years ahead of Patsy's, but I just forgot. And don't for God's sake tell her I called it the pensioner birthday – she'd never forgive me.'

'Oh, she won't mind,' said Storm and chuckled. 'She doesn't care about her age. You know her – she's looking forward to getting her pensioner card and getting on public transport at half price and all that, which is why she calls it a significant birthday. She's got no issues with getting older – very different from your mum, I imagine.'

It made Sofia smile to imagine her mother's reaction. 'God, yes! She wouldn't talk to me for a year if I said that in front of her. She thinks her career will come to an instant end if people find out her real age – she's officially been ten years younger than she really is for the last twenty years.' Then she laughed. 'I don't think she's ever checked the entry about herself on Wikipedia, which is what most people will do if they want to find out about her – they've got the right date of birth of course.'

They talked about other things for a few minutes and then Storm said he had to go, someone was waiting for him on Zoom, and Sofia put the phone beside her plate of now lukewarm food and thought about her strangely varied family. All talented in one way or another, but so different.

And that, she thought, was why the decision about how to handle this letter was such a conundrum. The obvious and honest option would be to put everything back in the envelope, deposit it safely in the archive at work and forget about it until her grandfather died. But if he died in the near future, say before her mother retired, then despite there being nobody to prosecute, her mother's fame would make it inevitable that media would leap on the story, because someone in the family wouldn't be able to resist making it public. Probably Fliss would, she thought. She would think it was fascinating and relish the attention and the drama that would follow if she posted it on social media, and she would probably claim she had always had a premonition or felt a spooky vibe in the house in Trentham as a child. And she might also think it would be good PR for her business, as if being a painter of portraits of people's dead pets from photographs needed some extra drama.

Storm would cope and probably think it was interesting in a weird way, but Summer would hate it. She was sensitive and uncertain about most things in life apart from her job. Sofia recalled the phrase Summer used once last year when they talked on the phone, talking about her reluctance to go to parties: "it's so unsettling when you can't work out what people think of you when you first meet them" Summer had said. Sofia found it incomprehensible, but also sad, that Summer was so insecure. There she was: a lecturer in biomedical genetics at the Otago medical school and owner of a lovely house on Maori Hill with views over a vast swathe of Dunedin, but so uncertain in social situations that she rarely finished a sentence. Becoming known to be connected to a drama in the sixties and the inevitable attention would devastate her.

The other option was to only put back in the envelope the little notes written by her grandparents, which contained no harmful information and leave the rest concealed for ever. If she could feel certain that nobody would suffer by the facts remaining hidden, that no descendants were being deprived of their family history, then she could square it with her conscience to do nothing.

It soon became clear that trying to sort the smaller notes into a time sequence was impossible because they were not dated, and the contents were too vaguely phrased to link one directly to another apart from a couple. She thought that this unvoiced conversation might well have covered some months, one person leaving a note for the other now and then, perhaps on the kitchen table and the other responding, maybe a day or two later. No exchange in person, a couple carrying on their daily life perhaps without ever sitting down and talking about things that were hard for both of them. But the love, she thought, the tenderness and the concern, how gentle and kind he was and how grateful she was; it brought tears to her eyes.

From photographs Patsy had, Sofia could picture her grandparents as a young couple, what they had looked like and how they dressed when her mother was a baby. They would both have been less than twenty-five and already had one small child and a baby and owned a house. Different times, she thought, a calmer, slower world without the complexities of the present. She went into the spare bedroom she used as a combination guest room and home office, scanned all the material on her printer and saved the resulting PDF file on her laptop. One day in the future, someone might open the file called "1962" and read it all, but it seemed unlikely. The smaller notes went back into her grandfather's envelope, which she sealed with tape and put to one side. The question of what to do with the two full-sized pages of writing could wait.

Chapter 6

I write this so someone in the future will know what happened. I came home from a Lions Club dinner at quarter to ten on Friday night (18 May) and there was no light in the house, which was strange. I used my key to go in the front door and called out for Glenys. She didn't answer but I could tell from the draught that the kitchen door was open, so I went to see if she was in the back garden, though it was dark and cold. She was sitting at the kitchen table in the dark. When I turned on the light, she didn't reply when I said her name, instead she pointed at the other side of the table. A man was lying on the floor in a pool of blood, that had come from his head, his temple was smashed right in, and he was dead and cold. On the floor beside him was our cast iron fry pan.

Glenys had put the children to bed and gone to the kitchen just on dusk to turn lights on and lock the back door. A man came in from the back and attacked her and threw her to the floor, but she managed to get up and quickly grabbed the fry pan that was on the bench to defend herself, but he came at her fast and she saw his flies were open. He was between her and the door to the garden and when he rushed at her, she swung the fry pan and hit his head. She had been sitting there in the dark for three hours and she was in a terrible state. It took me an hour to get out of her how it happened. I can't report it, I think it would destroy her, she has been so down ever since the baby was born and I don't think she could handle police and courts and such. I have already dug out what is going to be the concrete floor of the garage I'm building at the side of the house, and the shingle to mix the concrete was delivered on Wednesday along with the sacks of cement. I dragged the body into the laundry and locked the door. I know who he is, a beggar who has been in the town a short while. The next morning, I dug a much deeper hole in one part of the floor excavation as soon as the couple next door had gone out to play bowls as they always do on a Saturday. I put the body and the fry pan in the hole and then I fetched the concrete mixer from my neighbour on the other side as arranged and spent the rest of the weekend making the concrete floor and put the sprinkler on it to let it cure slowly. I will build the garage over the winter.

Angus Sylvester, 21 May 1962

. . .

I am writing this a year and a half after the first page I wrote. I feel I must explain my decision to conceal what happened and doing what I did, hiding the body and not telling anyone. At the time I acted on instinct, because I was so worried about Glenys and how it might affect her mental state and maybe leave our two little girls without a mother. Since then, I have found out from what people have said, that the vagrant was not known to have any connection to the town and nobody knew his full name, only that he told someone once to call him Bill and said that he had come from Manawatu. No enquiries seem to have been made about him and there has been nothing more than a short notice about him in the local paper just after he disappeared. The garage floor has held up well, with no cracks appearing where the body is in the NW corner where I put it in a deeper hole. I chose that corner so the weight of the car would never be right on top. Glenys is slowly coming right, and our little girls are thriving and happy and it makes me shudder to think how different it would all have been if I had reported it. I don't regret what I did. Glenys has accepted that it was an accident, she was defending herself and didn't intend to kill him, she just grabbed the first thing she saw to fend him off. I know I did wrong, but I don't regret it.

Angus Sylvester, 31 December 1963

The notes

"Stay calm today and remember it was an accident, and I

will never tell. Try to be cheerful with the girls, I'll put them to bed when I get home, Angus."

"Thank you for being so kind and patient. I know how lucky I am."

"Call the office if you feel down, you didn't get a lot of sleep. I'll bring something home and we can have lunch together."

"Don't worry about not keeping up with housework, it's not important. I can do things in the evenings. Kiss, Angus"

"Always wake me up if you worry about anything, you know I don't need a lot of sleep. I don't like to think of you sitting up at night alone. Angus"

"I can't say how safe you make me feel. I'm sorry I caused this. When I get better (really better) I will look after you!"

"Don't say you're sorry — it wasn't your fault. Try to think of it as something unfair that happened to you, not something for you to feel guilty about. I did what I did, it was my decision, and I don't regret it."

"It was lovely to come home and see you smiling again, it makes everything worthwhile for me."

"I smile inside every time I think of you."

"We are lucky to have each other. I think this last year has proven how strong we are."

"I love you. G"

Chapter 7

The call from Patsy on Sunday morning was predictably enervating and nearly instantly ruined Sofia's mood.

'What is it about this you don't understand, mum?' she said, trying to keep her voice from sounding impatient. 'It's perfectly simple, as I've already told you. A directly stated directive about a document to be kept under wraps until the writer is dead is something I *can't* ignore – lawyers have to be very careful about things like that. It's like client confidentiality, it's a must.'

'But who would know?' asked her mother, clearly thinking that this was a reasonable argument. 'There's no need to tell anyone, is there? Just open it and have a look and then seal it up again.'

Despite the fact that guilt over her own deceit

was now nearly choking her, Sofia interjected quickly, hoping to stem this flood of objections. 'But not when it's been formally registered as a lodged document and sealed with our company seal, mum! It simply can't be done. I had to pop in to work yesterday afternoon for a quick meeting with a client after I got back from Masterton and I put it in our vault, while I was there. Nobody can open it unless they present a death certificate to prove grandad is dead, it's just the way it is.'

The likelihood of her mother checking these exaggerated so-called facts, and the mention of 'formally registered' might close the argument.

'Oh, for God's sake!' said Patsy, disgruntled and impatient. 'All these damn rules! I don't know what the law has to do with it, it should be for the family to decide, but I suppose we'll just have to wait. And you're such a fusspot, Sofia, you always were – you're probably in the perfect job, all rules and regulations.'

'It's probably just his funeral wishes,' lied Sofia, ignoring the insults that were no worse than usual. 'These things are usually instructions for what kind of funeral someone wants, so I'll open it the moment he dies. And what about a birthday present for Fliss? We must give her something she'll really use, or something she needs. Not the kind of thing you and I would like, probably.'

'Oh, you do it, I don't care,' said Patsy carelessly, but Sofia knew that was an instruction not to be taken seriously, or there might be negative consequences one day in the future.

'I did think maybe a gift voucher to one of those speciality arts shops in Nelson or somewhere convenient – so she can buy quality paints and brushes or whatever she needs. What do you think?'

Much to her surprise, Patsy was instantly enthusiastic. 'Great idea! You get it organised and tell me how to refund you, straight into your bank account is probably the easiest. Let's make it two hundred dollars each, a decent amount.'

'OK, and I'll get a card for her from us both, but you've got to remember to call her on the day, too!'

They managed to end the call on what, for them, would be called good terms and Sofia made it to the Italian Food Festival only fifteen minutes late.

'Let's go back to the prosciutto stall, it's just by the entrance,' said Sian, when they found each other by exchanging texts. 'I love the stuff and I've been thinking about it ever since we tasted a piece when we arrived. I want to buy some. It keeps forever in a vacuum pack. You should taste it too, Sofia – perfect for someone like you who hates cooking, you just eat it as it is.'

After two hours of tasting cheeses, hams, olives and sausages at various stalls, and with a heavy shopping bag full of purchases, Barton suggested they have a late sushi lunch.

'What?!' exclaimed Sian, who often pretended to be shocked and amazed at things Barton said. 'Are you mad? Why would we lurch from one country to the other? Why don't we go to that Italian place we like? Keep up the atmosphere, so to speak.'

'I thought a complete change would be good, and we can't have lunch at Mr Go's with the kids, so it's an opportunity for us to have sushi,' said Barton, then turned to Sofia who had listened to this little exchange without contributing. 'If you don't mind, Sofia, but if we go there with the kids, they take hours to pick out what to have, piece by piece, and then they argue about what they ordered and start swapping and bargaining with each other and it's unbearable.'

Back in her apartment, Sofia decided to devote some time to researching the vagrant, who might or might not be called William, seeing he told someone to call him Bill. She tried every possible search description she could think of, adding spurious details at times to see what came up, but she found only two things. The mention in the Wairarapa Times, which was where the cutting had come from, and a small mention in an article from 2014, which described how in past decades drifters and beggars, usually men with no fixed abode, often seemed to simply disappear, possibly deciding just moving on from one town to the next, but never being remarked on again. A man called Bill, who for a year or two in the nineteen-fifties had been moving around Manawatu and Wairarapa, had disappeared out of view in this manner, but as with others, no record of his full name, or how or where he died could be found. How odd, she thought, to mention him at all, but maybe it was because he had already been mentioned in the Wairarapa paper, maybe the person who wrote the article came across that information and tried to find out more and failed.

Next, she decided to try to find out more about the man who had defrauded Mr Somerville, and much to her surprise she struck gold nearly immediately. The fact that he had used the assumed name, Erskine Frederick Greyson, in his role as a fraudster, inspired her to Google first that first name and then his initials, and finally Erskine F with and without the space. There was a ErskineF on

TradeMe,
 a person who was selling "a brand-new luxury motor home, only driven 2400 km and cost $210 000 when bought brand new."

'Gotcha!' said Sofia out loud and copied and saved the lot, the fourteen photos and the entire description that included a rather weak reason for selling something he had bought so recently. Of course, he wanted to sell it before a possible conviction, she thought, and then he would hide the money in some crypto currency so it couldn't be retrieved for poor Mr Somerville and he could still keep up the fiction that he'd gambled it away. With a cup of coffee beside her she decided to try for some extra detail, some identifying factor, so she called Storm.

'Hi,' she said breezily. 'Would you like to be my spy? It won't take long, but it will only work if you have a presence on TradeMe, but I can't be seen doing it. You do? Great! I'll tell you what I want you to do. Can you write this down, please? Find the entry titled "Practically new luxury motor home" – the seller is called ErskineF, no space, upper case letter F. Post a couple of questions, first something along the lines of "I'm very tall and don't want to have to bend, how high is the interior". And when he replies to that one, say "Very interested now, where are you located". I'll watch out for the answers. If he doesn't say how tall *he* is, ask him, say you want to compare. I'd like some additional detail about him, however insignificant.'

Storm laughed, and she could hear him tapping away at a keyboard. 'I'm at my laptop right now, actually - hang on a moment. Is this for a court case of something?'

She said, yes it was, and waited patiently until he exclaimed, 'Yes! Got it - I'm typing the first question as we speak. Are you going to tell me what this is about?'

'I will, but not until the case is over, so probably on Thursday when we have dinner together – if it works out.'

When Sofia checked TradeMe a couple of hours later, ErskineF had first replied, "I'm 6'4 and I have no problems, don't have to bend" and then, "You can pick it up in Fielding, I will text address if you provide phone number."

'Oh, no!' exclaimed Sofia out loud. 'Storm can't use his own number, it's an Australian one. I'll text him and say to respond and give my number.'

And then it was done; when Storm put Sofia's number on Erskine's TradeMe page, he texted the Fielding address to her phone.

After adding a screen shot of the questions and answers, and a last one of her phone with Erskine's address, she sent the file with all she had discovered to herself at work and went to bed. What a lucky thing that was, she thought, lying in bed listening to the rain pattering on the bedroom window. To get his address to add to everything else, I'll think we'll pull this off now, and dear, old Mr Somerville won't have to take the stand as a witness. A great day all round, apart from bumping into that damn Paul Strong at the food festival. I detest the way he mocks me, pretends to admire something I've achieved or something I've commented on in some legal forum, but it's like passive aggression, he's dismissing me as less than brilliant. He's been like that ever since the first case I was on where he was the prosecutor about eighteen months ago and I don't know why. Pity that someone so good-looking is so sarcastic.

Chapter 8

S hrugging out of her dripping coat as she passed
Clare's desk, Sofia made a face. 'What a
shocker of a day!' she said. 'I took the bus instead of
walking, and I still got totally drenched.'

Clare followed her and held out four pink memo
notes. 'I'll take your coat and hang it outside the
lunchroom, it's too wet for you to have it in here. You
must get on to these two messages marked urgent
before you set out for the court. Mr Somerville is
quite frantic about his appearance and says he needs
to check a couple of things with you. I think he wants
to take some notes he's made into the witness box.
The poor man is terrified that nobody is going to
believe him or that he's going to get muddled and
trip himself up.'

'OK, I will.' Sofia opened her briefcase and got

the envelope out. 'I talked to my mum yesterday and said I've already put this envelope in our archive, and I can't legally go against my grandfather's wishes and open it – which is what she wanted me to do. So, we'd better get it into the archive right away. She found it very hard to accept that we can't do whatever she wants, even if granddad said to keep it until he's dead. I did *not* tell her that there aren't any directions on the envelope itself or she would have started an argument, but he told me several times what he wanted me to do with it.'

'Maybe you could write up a little contract and get him to sign it - or get him to sign the outside of the envelope saying what his wishes are.'

'No, I'm afraid we can't. By the time I finally found the damn thing he'd already forgotten about it again – he'll remember it again one day, but there was no way I could draw up anything for him to sign, he's not legally competent to sign anything. So, I told mum that it's entered it in the client database where we list all the documents we hold for clients, and that we can't go against his wishes - and she won't know whether he wrote the instructions on it or not.'

'Just let me jot down his full name and address or perhaps we can make it c/o your address - I'll do it now. What's the item called? Shall we call it a will?'

Sofia laughed. 'Your guess is as good as mine,

Clare. I've no idea what's inside it, but let's call it funeral instructions. His name is Angus Sylvester. I suggest you find another big envelope and seal his one inside - and I'll write the details on the outside of how I got it, date and sign it, then you can witness it and put it away.'

Sofia made two calls before she had to leave the office to go to the court. The first one to the defence lawyer for the man who had used the name Erskine Greyson, but who was really called Warwick Harmer, was brief and satisfying.

'I'll send you the file with the TradeMe post and my suggestions for restitution,' she said after explaining what she had found. 'And if your client agrees with my demands in writing and changes his plea to guilty, we can finish the case this morning. I would like to avoid having to get a forfeiture order, because it takes forever and sometimes doesn't work very well. And what I'm suggesting would be so simple – all he has to do is withdraw the motor home from being on sale and change the ownership in the vehicle register to my client. Much simpler than anything else and it's just about the exact sum he stole. It does depend on no bids having been made on it by then, of course, but right now there aren't any, I checked just a few minutes ago.'

The second call was to the company from whom the fraudster had bought the motor home, a fact he had conveniently put on his TradeMe post, and then it was time to go to the courthouse.

A few hours later, Mr Somerville hugged Sofia with tears running down his cheeks, overcome by emotion. 'It's like a miracle,' he sobbed and held her tight, his skinny old arms like steel bands around her. 'I thought I'd never get the money back, but now I'll be able to sleep again. I'll figure out how to sell the van and then it's done.'

'Let's go to that café down the street and have a coffee and a very, very late lunch to celebrate,' said Sofia, liberating herself from his grip and turning to pick up her papers from the table. 'I have time now that's it's over so quickly. I want to explain a couple of things to you, just to make sure it all works really well.'

Not what she normally did, after a case, but with Mr Somerville so old, and with little idea how to manage the sale of the motorhome, she thought maybe she could help him a bit.

'It seems like a miracle, it really does,' said Mr Somerville again, when they had ordered and were waiting for their lunch to arrive. 'I never thought I'd get the full amount back. You read about fraudsters having spent half the money and there's nothing to show for it that can be sold – or they just gamble it away. I just have to figure out how to sell the damn thing.'

'That's what I want to tell you about,' said Sofia and smiled at the old man who had been transformed into a different man than he had been up to now. Having a smile on his face turned him into someone ten years younger, a hopeful and positive old man instead of someone who had nearly given up on life.

'So, this is what I did before I went to the court - I called the firm in New Plymouth that the thief bought the motor home from and explained to their manager what had happened. I suggested that as a gesture of goodwill to an old man who had been ripped off, they could buy it back for the purchase price less a small amount for the couple of thousand kilometres it had been driven since new. I pointed out that doing a good deed might be good PR for the company, which they could use on their website if the wanted to - and to my surprise he agreed. So now that you have ownership of it you can sell it back to them.'

'Have I got ownership of it right now? Was that what we did on your computer with the other lawyer and the thief and the judge? I wasn't quite sure that was it – it's interesting how things are so easy now, isn't it?' And then he laughed. 'If you know how to do it!' She nodded because his expression was the best reward she could have – that beaming smile, lovely!

'And my son will help me,' said Mr Somerville. 'You know how that scumbag said I had to come and pick it up? Well, I don't want to do that, not on my own. I've never driven a thing that big in my life. When I saw the photos you had I couldn't believe it – it's huge! But my son will do it for me, and I'm sure he'll drive it to New Plymouth too, to sell it back to that company.'

'Excellent,' said Sofia and studied her plate the waitress had just put in front of her. 'Would you look at this omelette, it's nearly as big as that motor home! But you have to go with your son, perhaps drive over in convoy, so you have something to come back in too, because it's got to be you transferring the ownership after they've paid you for it. And make sure you insure it before you even drive it away from that thief's property and then you cancel the insurance once the dealer has bought it back from you.'

Mr Somerville looked slightly overwhelmed by all the instructions and said, 'Would you be able to write all that down for me, just in case I forget. So, I can check it off and feel sure we've done it all right? If you send it to me, I'll show it to my son.'

They parted outside an hour later and as she watched Mr Somerville walk away, Sofia's mind was already on what she wanted to achieve now she had an unexpected couple of hours free that afternoon.

Chapter 9

Making her way to The Old Bailey bar to meet Helen for a drink after work seemed more like an obstacle race than a fifteen-minute walk. The flow of pedestrians hurrying towards Willis Street and weaving between others heading for the railway station made it hard to stay on course, and Sofia resorted to walking as close to the buildings as she could to avoid being pushed aside or buffeted by briefcases.

'It's on the harbour side of the street in that building that has a kind of dome with multi-coloured windows – you know the one. Or just look for the barrels,' Helen had said when Sofia confessed she didn't know where the bar was. 'It looks like a beer and scotch drinkers' paradise, but it's actually very nice. Oscar and I have a drink there quite often and sometimes we stay for a basic but tasty dinner. I'll try to get a table down at the fireplace end where people don't push past you all the time.'

Amazing, thought Sofia, when she went up the steps to the door at The Old Bailey, but I've never really registered the fact this place is here. If I ever venture all the way down here I mostly walk on the other side of the street and I'm looking straight ahead.'

Helen waved from a table for two in the corner by the stone fireplace and pointed at her glass and then at the bar, so Sofia bought a glass of white wine before she joined her.

'I didn't realise it was all the way down here,' she said accusingly. 'You said it was just down the street from your office, but it's a mile further on. I've never noticed it before, I always walk on the other side of the street.'

'Where are you on your way to down this end of town? Parliament, railway station?' Helen grinned. 'It's past the end of the shopping part of the CBD.'

'National Archives, actually. Despite the Internet and all it can provide, sometimes I have to research something in person. And I love the place – full of secrets and treasures hidden away from the superficial stuff you get when you Google. Or most of the time. Did you order some bar snacks, or should I do it? I'm starving.'

'I've ordered bread, cheese, ham and olives and then we have the choice of some tapas type stuff or a proper meal.' Helen pushed her glass across the table. 'Have a sip of that and tell me what you think.'

'Nice!' Sofia took another sip. 'Very nice. When did you take up drinking beer?'

Helen waited while their snack was put on the table and took another sip of her glass. 'It's zero percent alcohol beer – well, it's not zero, it's about half a percent. I like that kind of lemony background taste. One of the women at work is laying off wine and she said she drinks this instead. I think it's going to become my regular drink at the start of an evening, lessen the total alcohol consumption.'

'Where's Oscar?'

Helen made a face. 'More after school activities, and this lot takes place in the evening once a week. Try not to laugh – he's in a play! Persuaded by the drama teacher, who's a very persuasive guy, very intense. I've only met him once and I was exhausted after ten minutes.'

Having known Oscar for four or five years, Sofia found it hard to imagine him involved in acting. 'But he's so into everything physical, he's a real sportsman! Not that it precludes acting talent, but it just seems … surprising.'

'Totally! It surprised me too, but he's enjoying it. His part is a clergyman! Bet you didn't expect that.' She laughs at Sofia's expression. 'You might well be amused, but he's right into it now, says he never realised how exciting it is to be someone else, who's completely different. I can kind of see what he means, but sometimes it seems like a personality transplant, probably the last thing I'd ever think he would be likely to agree to.'

'Mm,' said Sofia around a piece of cheese she had just put in her mouth. 'Like being an undercover cop, playing at being someone else. I find it hard to picture him as clergy. What's the play?'

'It's called the Crucible – about the Salem witch-trials. It's sounds dire but I'll have to go and watch it, I suppose. Apparently there's often a male role they can't fill in those school productions, so they resort to a parent or one of the staff, and for some reason Oscar agreed.'

'I'll tell you something I discovered a few weeks ago when I went to look for something at the National archives,' said Sofia. 'You know how you like reading thrillers – well, here's something just for you. I was in there and I asked a staff member I was chatting to what the most intriguing things they every found was, and she said she herself found a murder weapon in a box of old court records a few years ago! A knife that had been evidence in a murder trial decades ago!'

'You're kidding!' said Helen and started to laugh. 'Surely they don't have stuff like that in the archives.'

'Well, they did have that one, but they didn't know it was in among all those old papers until this woman found it. And guess who she is when she's not an archivist? She's a thriller writer in her spare time!'

They toasted the woman who found the knife and the conversation morphed into a discussion of books and why Sofia rarely read a crime novel. 'So, what are you reading at the moment?' asked Helen. 'You're reading habits are so random, I never know what to expect.'

'Oh, a great trilogy of books called Ender's Game – riveting. I've never read science fiction before. It's not new, but it was mentioned in an article I read online, so I got the ebook version. It's got me hooked.'

Helen grinned and raised her glass in a toast. 'It's one of Oscar's favourites too – he re-read it last year I think it was and told me I should read it. I might do it now that you've recommended it too.'

. . .

An hour later they ordered dinner and Helen returned from a visit to the Ladies with a stressed looking stranger in tow.

'Sofia, this is Gabriel – he needs a bit of help, and I thought your French would do better than my pathetic attempts.'

By the time their meal was set in front of them, Sofia had solved Gabriel's problem with the help of both their cell phones and some detective work on Sofia' part. He left with the place marked on his Navigate app, a much happier man.

'So, what was that all about?' said Helen and reached for the saltshaker. 'I didn't understand more than a word here and there – you both talked too fast, and my schoolgirl French isn't up to it. I take it he'd somehow forgotten where he was staying? Or did I get that wrong? It must be terrible to be in a country where you barely speak the language – and then get lost.'

'His travelling companion speaks fluent English, but for some reason they parted in the centre of town somewhere after lunch, and Gabriel thought he'd be able to find his way back to their B&B without having the address. Poor chap - he sent a text to his friend but got no answer, but he had emails on his phone, so we found the message with the address from a couple of weeks ago and I downloaded the

Navigate app and put the address in there for him.' She grinned at Helen, 'He said, "but the streets are all curved here, nothing is at right angles, and I was lost" – isn't that funny. I never thought of it before, but we do have lots of curving streets in Wellington.' And then she added, 'My father's name was Gabriel.'

Later that evening as they stood looking into a shoe shop window on their way home, Helen said, 'How long is it since you saw your French family? Covid must have stuffed up your plans – weren't you just about to go when we had the first lock-down?'

'I cancelled it before the situation was quite clear, before the big lockdown had been flagged as even a possibility. I had this awful feeling that things were going to get pear-shaped in Europe, and I thought I might not get back. Isn't it odd, we've never had the country locked up before, but that's what I worried about. Borders closing, travel shut down and all kind of hassle. Not that it would have been a catastrophe for me, I've got uncles and aunts and cousins who would have put me up indefinitely, but now it seems incredible.'

Helen pushed her with her elbow. 'What seems incredible? Don't stop there, I don't know what you mean.'

'I mean that worrying it would be hard to get back was a bit uncanny, like a prediction. Because I really did think they might close the borders, and that's what it turned into, quarantine hotels, having to practically go into a lottery for flights back, people waiting months and months. It was very lucky. But I think I'll go in May next year - spring in Paris, lovely!'

Chapter 10

A couple of days later Clare came into Sofia's room and said apologetically, 'I'm so sorry! I've totally stuffed up your day. I didn't check if you had entered anything yourself since I last looked at your diary and now you don't have a lunch hour. Maybe I can call them back and change it? Or I could go out and pick something up for you to eat before you see them.'

'Who is it?'

'Mr Bradley – he said it's about the scholarship he's setting up and he's bringing his wife and son.'

'Oh God, no, don't try to change it. He's such an old fusspot, I'd better see him, or I'll never hear the last of it. Have I got anything between now and twelve?' Sofia turned to her laptop. 'No, I've got an hour and fifteen minutes, so I'll go out and have a very early lunch or maybe it will be brunch.' Noticing how embarrassed Clare looked, she added, 'It's probably perfect – too early for the crowds so I won't have to wait, don't worry about it.'

She was in the cafe doorway, her right hand holding the door when a man appeared from inside and as he pushed past her, and her hand caught in the doorhandle. With a yelp of pain, she pulled it free and stared shocked at her little finger, which was sticking out at a seemingly impossible angle. Feeling slightly sick and gripping her right wrist tightly with her left hand, she took a couple of steps further in and turned her back to the counter, not wanting anyone to see that her eyes were full of tears. The pain was intense, and she couldn't think of what to do. She had an irrational feeling that if she let go of her wrist, the weight of the unsupported, damaged hand would overwhelm her. She let out a small groan of pain and fear. Then hands gripped her upper arms firmly from behind and moved her to the side. 'Sit down here,' said a familiar voice and she only had time to think *Paul Strong* before he pushed her down on a chair by the window table.

'You look as if you're about to fall over.' He pulled the second chair over to sit at right angles to her and put one of his hands under hers. 'Let go now, I've got your hand – just keep still.'

He moved the finger which sent a shock of pain down the side of the hand and made her groan again. 'Sorry,' he said and did it again in a different place, and then again. 'I don't think it's broken, just dislocated. I'll put it back – clench your teeth and don't look.'

Obediently she looked out of the window beside her and bit back another groan as he did something excruciatingly painful to her finger. Still supporting her hand with one of his, he put a finger on her chin and turned her face towards him, studied her face. 'Good girl – I don't think you're going to faint. Don't touch that finger, I'll be back in a moment.'

He rested her hand on the table and went to the counter, and she watched with a strange sense of detachment as he pulled a waitress to one side, gestured at Sofia and talked intently to her. The woman glanced over, nodded and disappeared out the back, while Sofia looked down at her hand and suddenly felt like crying. Though her finger was no longer at an angle, it was swelling as she watched it, and the pain was as bad as ever.

'Here we are.' Paul put a red box on the table and opened it, talking quite casually while he searched through it. 'That's usually done with a local anaesthetic, but the sooner it's back in place the better, so I thought we might as well do it right away. Ah, this will do.'

Putting a roll of wide tape on the table he returned his attention to the box and found a pair of scissors. Once again, he reached over and put a finger under her chin to raise her face to look directly at him. 'I'm sorry - I'm going to hurt you again, but this won't take long. Look at me, not at your hand. It always hurts more if you watch what's being done.'

Sofia felt her eyes fill with tears. 'Pain?' he said. 'And scared?'

Not trusting here voice, she nodded and thought that she could never tell him why she had nearly cried. The feeling that his finger on her chin had left a warm mark, that she was being looked after and cared for, was nearly too private to even think about. It was a feeling she had not experienced to this extent since she was a tiny girl, when her father was alive. And this man didn't really care for her, he was just helping.

'Just hold on now – you'll feel a lot better soon.'

She nodded again and instead of keeping her eyes on his face, she watched as he cut three short lengths of tape, attached them to the edge of the first aid box and picked up a wooden coffee stirrer she hadn't noticed. Breaking the stirrer to shorten it, he put it between her ring finger and the little finger and strapped them together, and nearly instantly she felt safe again, though it was still painful. Realising that she had not said a single word since it happened, she opened her mouth to thank him, but he cut in before she got a word out.

'Stay here, I won't be long.'

Again, she watched him go to the counter where he seemed to place an order, then he handed the box to the woman he had already talked to, said something that made her laugh and returned to the table.

'I've ordered coffee and something to eat – something sweet will be good for you. And they're giving us some painkillers that you can take with your coffee. It's still painful, isn't it?'

She could only stare at him, nearly overwhelmed by this swift, competent response to her injury. 'Thank you! I'm sorry I was so shocked and useless – it just happened so fast – and it looked so … grotesque.'

He grinned. 'It might not be over yet – you should probably see your doctor, just to be on the safe side, but I'm pretty sure it's going to be ok. Some ligaments stretched and needing a rest, but nothing serious, I don't think. That kind of sudden intense pain puts most people into a state of light shock, but you'll feel better when we get those painkillers into you and you eat something – oh, here we are.'

The waitress put a glass of water, four painkillers in tinfoil and a plastic bag of ice cubes in front of Sofia, patted her shoulder and said, 'Take a couple these and I'll bring your order – I'm very sorry this happened to you.'

Sofia, still slow to react, watched Paul flip out two capsules and hold his hand out. 'Here – you can swallow capsules, I hope?'

When coffee and almond croissants were put in front of them, normality finally seemed to have returned and Sofia felt calmer. With the side of her hand resting on the bag of ice she said, 'How did you know how to do all that? I had no idea what to do.'

'Believe it or not, I was a paramedic before I studied law and it's been useful more than once. Eat that croissant now and get some sugar into you, it will make you feel better.'

Impulsively she reached over with her undamaged hand and curled her fingers briefly around his. 'I can't tell you how grateful I am you were here! Like magic.'

From the ironic look he gave her she knew what he was thinking; he was remembering all the occasions when she had treated him coldly and suddenly she wondered if she had misread him ever since they first met on a case a couple of years earlier. Had he been mocking her, or had she just imagined it? She studied his face in silence and he made no response to her comment, just looked back without expression, and then she started to laugh. 'You know what? It's your eyebrows!'

'What? My eyebrows?'

'I've always thought you were mocking me, being sarcastic – even when you said something that sounded nice, as if it was a trick.'

She looked intently at his face, tried to imagine him with straighter or curved brows. 'But you didn't, did you? Mock me, I mean. It's the way your eyebrows have that devilish upward slant, it gives you a sarcastic look.'

'Jesus! What a thing to find out about myself at my age! Of course, I never meant to mock you – why on earth would I?' He thought for a moment and said thoughtfully. 'But I must admit I've often wondered what you had against me, that coolness, polite but chilly, it was quite unnerving at times.'

They spent half an hour over coffee with some more or less ordinary conversation. She told him about the aborted Somerville trial and the happy outcome, and it turned out he knew already, which surprised her, such a short and undramatic case and no media attention.

'I sat in on it for a few minutes,' he said with a measuring look. 'I had a few minutes between cases, and I struck it lucky, walked in just as the judge was explaining to the jury how it had been resolved, before he dismissed them. I'm not being sarcastic - please remember it's just my eyebrows – but I was interested. I've often popped in to hear you in court, just when I have half an hour or so, when I'm moving around the courthouse.'

'Really? But why?' She was taken aback, and she could hear her voice sounding nearly alarmed. 'Do you just pop in and out of random court rooms, to see what's going on?' Or are you keeping an eye on me, she thought, checking my performance for some reason?

The corner of his mouth tweaked up a fraction. 'Nothing random about it – I just enjoy listening to you. Clear, concise, undramatic – a masterclass in court delivery, very effective. When I've managed to catch you in action, I watched the jury while you speak and it's clear you reach them like few others do.'

She was speechless, both at the revelation that he

had been watching her for some time, but also at the unexpected praise. Instead of responding with something that directly related to what he said, she confessed something she never talked about.

'Sometimes, in a closing argument I just ad-lib. I ditch everything I had planned to put forward, ignore my notes and just say what I feel, what I genuinely believe the jurors should remember and consider before they reach a decision.'

'I know, I can tell when you do that, I can hear it in your voice - and it's very effective. It comes across as totally genuine, that it's something you really believe, and the jury can hear that.'

When they parted outside, he took a step away after she thanked him once again, but then he turned. 'Would you mind giving me your phone number – now that you know it's just the eyebrows?'

It made her laugh, the way he said that, like a private, shared joke nobody else would understand. She gave him her number and said, 'Send me a text and I'll save yours too.'

Her phone pinged in her bag as she walked back to the office, but she ignored it and kept her right hand against her chest to avoid anyone bumping into it. The strapped finger throbbed, but she was able to ignore it and thought how lucky it was that he had been there just at the right moment.

Chapter 12

That night Sofia dreamt she was sitting on a beach with a spade in her hand, confused and frightened, as people gathered around something she couldn't see at the water's edge. She got up to see what they were doing, but someone took hold of her arm and held her back, saying, 'Non, non, cherie – tu devrais rester ici avec moi' repeatedly.

She woke with her heart beating fast, just the way it had that day on the beach at Donville-les-Bains when her father drowned. How confused and frightened she had felt when that stranger told her she should stay with him, when all she wanted to do was to see what it was they were looking at down by the water's edge. She got up, made a mug of hot chocolate, and sat in her favourite little armchair by the bedroom window thinking about the father she had so few memories of.

Long after the event, when she was a teenager, she pieced together the details that she had been too young to know or understand at the time. She heard her mother tell the story, and she once listened to her grandmother telling two friends about it, when Patsy had left her with her grandparents for a couple of weeks when she was eleven. Over the years the whole story came together as a whole, but she herself had only told it once, when her friend Helen asked where the Garnier surname came from.

The year Sofia turned four, her mother she was engaged to sing in two productions with at the opera in Lyon and was there for early rehearsals in September, though the season would not start until later. Her father was between engagements and looked after her for several weeks, and they went to spend a week with friends in a holiday cottage on the Normandy coast where they had all stayed the previous summer. Sofia remembered vividly the wife of the couple, who had very long dark hair that Sofia was allowed to brush, standing behind the tilted-back deckchair in the slanting late afternoon sun with the men sitting in the shade with drinks in their hands. She remembered the stone-flag floor with shell fossils in the stone slabs in the cottage passage and kitchen, and the funny black pot-bellied stove. She could feel the hot sand under her feet as she stood watching as her father and the other man, whose name she could no longer remember, assembled their windsurfers and got into their wetsuits, and then how they seemed to nearly fly over the waves in sprays of water, faster than the boats.

She herself didn't see the accident, she was too busy building a sandcastle with a moat, with the woman with the long dark hair lying on her back on a towel beside her reading a book that she held above her with straight arms, so it shadowed her face. When the commotion and the shouts broke out the woman sat up, threw the book to one side and ran towards the water. Sofia got up and stared after her, then followed slowly, but someone took hold of her arm and lifted her up, held her tight. An urgent voice she didn't know told her, 'Non, non, cherie – reste ici avec moi'. And so she watched, confused and frightened, held by a stranger as her father died surrounded by a crowd, and she never saw him again.

When she was told this story, Helen, aged ten, had put her arms around Sofia, right there on the little grassed hill in the school's so-called quiet area, where they were not allowed to run or shout.

'You poor little thing,' she said, as if they were not exactly the same age, and they sat like that until the bell went and never talked about it again. Helen was always like that, thought Sofia, a bit like a mother, so kind and lovely, and she still is, of course.

Half an hour later she went back to bed, surprised at the number of French phrases and words that popped up in her head. Not the everyday conversational ones she used on her visits to France and with her French family, but rhymes and word games her father used to play with her, and the silly phrases he and she used when they played games or went out on a Saturday morning to buy croissants and a baguette. The pretend words they made up to describe the ugly baker and the woman who sold flowers on the corner. It's like archaeological finds from a distant past, she thought. Perhaps it's true that we never forget anything, we just lose the link to some memories.

The last conscious thought she had before she fell asleep again was that perhaps Patsy did believe that Sofia could remember the day her father died, but she didn't want to talk about it. Perhaps she somehow felt guilty that she had not been there that

September day, or maybe she was jealous that Sofia had been present without her.

In the morning she didn't listen to the news as she usually did but lay repeating those rhymes and play-words until she was certain she wouldn't forget them again. A link to her past, just like she had felt when she found their apartment building in Paris on Google Earth and recognised the crooked tree that grew on the pavement outside. The apartment windows had looked down on that tree and she still remembered the birds' nests she counted from her bedroom in the autumn when the leaves had fallen, sitting on the deep window ledge surrounded by her dolls.

Chapter 13

Anything celebrated at Logan Brown becomes better than it would be nearly anywhere else, thought Sofia, as she entered the impressive domed space. She hoped they would have the table in the alcove on the far right, the one with that moody painting, which was her favourite. She glanced across the room and there they were with Storm waving, and as she made her way towards him, she realised he had brought his children.

Greetings and hugs took some time, and Sofia thought how amazing it was that Christina and Gregory, whom she had last seen only two years ago, when they were twelve and thirteen suddenly seemed like young adults. Gone were the hugs with arms wound tight around her and the competition to be the first to tell her things; instead, they embraced her gently, kissed her cheek and then went back to talking between themselves.

'I can't get over it,' she said to Storm when they were seated again. 'How on earth did this happen? They seem to have matured five years in the two since I last saw them.'

'Don't ask me! I have to remind myself to behave when I'm with them in public these days. Daddy kissing them goodbye is only marginally accepted, and never outside their school - and ruffling their hair is totally *verboten*. I think Greg takes longer to arrange his hair in the morning than Christina does.'

Sofia laughed at Gregory's moan of 'Dad!' and said, 'Don't mind him, Greg – if you put up with him for another five years or so, you'll probably discover he's a great guy.'

'And now we're all *finally* sitting down, let's get them to bring the champagne so we can toast mum and wish her a happy birthday.'

While the initial chaos had been going on, Sofia had glanced at Summer, who as usual quietly watched and listened without contributing much, but with a smile. Green hair! thought Sofia, how surprising, probably the last thing I would have expected from Summer. And that black top, *very* unlike anything I've ever seen her wear before, overtly sexy. I wonder what caused this change.

'What happened to your finger?' asked Christina, who was seated next to Sofia. 'Did you break it? Is it sore?'

'It was very sore to start with, but it's feeling a lot better now. I got it caught in a doorhandle at a café and it wrenched itself out of joint. You should have seen it – gross! It stuck out at a horrible angle.'

'How did they fix it? Did they operate on it?'

'Oh, no – an ambulance guy, who happened to be in the café at the time, just took hold of it and said, "clamp your teeth together, this will hurt" and put it back into place.'

Christina looked shocked, and Sofia laughed and reached over to pat her hand. 'It only took a second and I did moan and groan a bit, but it was over in a flash.'

An hour later Fliss leaned towards Sofia and spoke softly, while the others were laughing at one of Storms made-up stories about how atrocious his children were.

'Have you met Summer's new girlfriend? No? Neither have I, but she's moved in and they're talking about getting married. She's changed – for the better. I'm not sure I like her wearing black, but I suppose now she's got green hair it's OK.'

'I like the top, and the green hair – it adds colour,' said Sofia and smiled at Fliss, who was dressed in a dark red velvet kaftan that nearly matched her current hair colour. 'I'm really happy for her.'

'Any men on the horizon?' asked Fliss in a sudden brief moment of silence, and four pairs of eyes swivelled to study Sofia, who had been expecting that Fliss would sooner or later probe into her life, the way she always did. 'You're not getting any younger, you know. Thirty-four on your next birthday?'

'Thirty-three,' said Sofia, 'and no, no particular man on the scene but it doesn't worry me.'

Summer shot her a sympathetic glance and shook her head at this approach from her mother; very familiar as she had been subjected to it for several years herself.

Gregory stared hard at his grandmother and said, 'You shouldn't ask people things like that, grandma, not in public – it's embarrassing.'

Then he blushed beetroot red and looked down at his plate and Sofia said, 'Thank you for defending me, Greg! I don't think I've ever had anyone in my corner on this subject before. They've all been nagging about it for the last five years. If you take my advice, ignore people who nag at you about getting married or having babies and do your own thing.'

Gregory raised his head and smiled his father's wide smile. 'Oh, I will, don't worry. I'm not getting into any of that stuff until I'm ready – I won't have time. I'll have a career to look after, just like you.'

Storm looked from Greg to Sofia and back again and said, 'My God, Sofe – you've made him reveal he has plans for his future – I never heard him say anything like that before.'

'Of course not,' said Sofia. 'You're his father, for God's sake – he's not going to confide in you until he needs you to fund his university fees.' Turning to Gregory she asked, 'What have you got planned – I mean, what kind of career?'

To hers and everybody's surprise Gregory said confidently, 'I'm going to do aerospace engineering. I want to go to Monash first and then to MIT in the US for my masters if I can get in.'

'Great!' said Sophia and tried not to laugh at the expression on Storm's face. 'There's nothing like having a plan. I think I was about your age when I decided what I was going to do, and it always amazed me that a lot of the kids I went to school with thought that was weird.'

When Fliss mentioned over dessert that they were going to drive to Masterton the next day to visit her father, Sofia grasped the opportunity. 'I saw him recently – you'll probably find him a bit more muddled than he was last time you came. He keeps losing things and he thought someone had stolen a letter he wanted to give me, but it was in his bedside cabinet – he'd used it as a drawer liner!'

'For goodness' sake,' said Fliss. 'Has he got that bad all of a sudden? I saw him a few months ago and he seemed quite with it, I thought. Mind you, he's not far off ninety and dementia comes and goes a bit, doesn't it? He might just have had a good day when I was there. What was the letter about?'

'I've no idea – it's sealed, and he wants me to keep it safe until he dies, so I put it in the archive at work.' And as if to demonstrate how utterly different she was from Sofia's mother, Fliss asked no further questions about the letter. Sofia thought how strange it was to find that Fliss had been in Wellington so recently and she hadn't known and wondered if Storm and Summer hadn't known either when they decided to give her a trip to Wellington for a birthday present. But Fliss as always different, she thought, impulsive and a bit random and had always lived a very bohemian life.

While Storm explained to his children why he loved driving over the ranges on the Remutaka road, Sofia took the opportunity to ask Fliss for the address where she and Patsy had grown up. 'Grandad was saying he hadn't seen the place for years, so I thought I'd go and take a picture of it next time I go and visit him. I know it was in Trentham, but I don't know the actual address.'

'I'll text it to you,' said Fliss. 'I just need to think a bit, I know the street of course, but I can't remember if it was forty-three or forty-five. When you're a kid, that kind of detail doesn't really matter, but it will come to me. I'll park it in the back of my mind.'

Sofia turned down an offer of sharing a taxi van and was walking home to her apartment on Taranaki Street when her phone buzzed, and she stopped to see who texted so late. 'Would you like to meet for a drink tomorrow after work? Paul'

Brief and to the point, she thought, and replied 'Of course – tell me time and place and I'll be there.'

Chapter 14

As soon as they sat down at a table in the Merchant the next night, she noticed Paul glancing at her hand.

'Is that the strapping I put on it the other day? Didn't you go to the doctor?'

'It felt so much better the next day I thought I'd save myself the trouble.' She saw the frown and added quickly. 'It's true, it feels quite good. I thought it was a bit like a cast, you know – leave it on until it's healed.'

He shook his head, as if he couldn't believe she could be so careless. 'For God's sake – I need to get that off and have a look. And how did you keep it dry?'

'Plastic bag,' she said calmly. 'And a rubber band. It worked fine.'

'Well, we'll soon check that. You stay here and drink your wine and I'll be back in fifteen minutes. And don't you go away and think you can avoid this – I'm not joking, Sofia!'

She laughed quietly as she watched him walk down the length of the room and out the door and told herself she knew where he was going as surely as if she was watching him from a drone. He'd walk around the corner of Courtenay Place to the New World supermarket and return with everything he needed. A hundred bucks I'm right, she thought, scissors, tape and whatever. Not a man to be fobbed off, set on doing what he feels is the right thing and issuing orders to make me comply.

Hard-earned experience had left her determined to never again put up with men, who told her what to do, but the way he told her stay where she was, as if he had a right to do it, made her feel warm and looked after. He didn't do it because he felt superior or thought he knew better, it was more as if he wanted to make sure she was all right, safe and cared for. It was a new experience for Sofia, something that felt surprisingly pleasant. I don't have anyone who does that kind of thing for me, she thought, perhaps it's because I'm so determined and a bit bossy – nobody thinks I need taking care of now and then, apart from Helen sometimes.

When Paul arrived back, she was reading the news on her phone and had a nearly empty glass of wine in front of her. 'I've just asked them to bring a bowl of fries and some other stuff a minute ago. It should give us time to get on with the torture session first. And they'll bring me another glass of wine and you a new glass of beer – you know, so you get it all new and cold, with the bubbles intact.'

'Thank you,' he said politely, 'but let's get this done first.' He took a blue tape dispenser with a roll of tape that looked like paper out of his pocket and a little white box with a picture of a finger on it. 'I'll have to ask them if they can lend me a pair of scissors, just a moment.'

The process of getting the tape off her hand tested her composure despite how careful he was, and she gritted her teeth to avoid a groan escaping. The fingers she hadn't seen for three days looked very pale and slightly deformed.

'They look squished,' she said. 'Do you think that finger is kind of swollen but compressed, or is it just that it's a bit misshapen now?'

He didn't reply, just said, 'Right – this might hurt, sorry!' and took hold of her little finger and moved it around slowly, and she bit back a gasp and tried not to flinch. Paul looked up and smiled. 'Good girl! I think it's going to be fine. Just keep it strapped another couple of days, the pain won't last long.'

She watched as he cut a short length of tubular bandage and slid it over her little finger and again strapped the two fingers together with the white tape but without the wooden coffee stirrer and thought she couldn't remember anyone ever saying, "good girl!" to her in exactly that tone of voice.

'Right,' he said again. 'That will be a lot easier to get off than that thick tape they had at the café. And now this - hold your hand up.'

Out of his other pocket came a roll of narrow brown bandage, and as Sofia watched him cut a length off, she wondered what would next appear as if by magic. With the brown bandage firmly wrapped around the two fingers and anchored at the wrist, he pushed the things in front of him to one side just as a waiter arrived with their order.

Sofia looked at the now much neater parcel of strapped-together fingers, flexed them slightly and smiled. Once again, she reached out and curled the fingers of her other hand around his, but this time she didn't pull her hand back straight away.

'I'm so lucky,' she said quietly, 'and I hope you realise that I know it. I've done nothing to deserve how kind you've been and how you've helped me and looked after me.'

For a long silent moment, he studied her face, then he lifted her hand off his and kissed her knuckles. 'It was a pleasure.'

Chapter 15

Lying dreamily in bed the next morning, Sofia thought what a blessing it was to live in a modern apartment where double glazing admitted none of the traffic noise from Taranaki Street three floors down. She lifted her bandaged hand and gently prodded the wrapped-up little finger and felt hardly any pain. Seeing the undamaged hand suspended above her face made her remember the little incident the previous day, the way Paul had kissed her hand. Such an unusual thing to do; nobody had ever kissed her knuckles before. It seemed like a formal and old-fashioned caress, and it had made her feel a multitude of emotions at the same time: surprise, a charge of warmth travelling up her arm and a shiver of something, maybe lust.

And how will it be now, she thought, next time

we meet? Will I get that feeling again that I had last night, when I kept looking at his hands, wanting to feel them on me again, strong and capable and warm. An unfamiliar urge, whatever it was. I can't believe the effect it had on me, that feeling of being cared for and looked after and able to totally trust someone else's judgment, it's not a bit how I am normally. The reverie was broken by her phone buzzing on the bedside table, Sian calling.

'Hi,' said Sian. 'Just to warn you, I've got the phone on speaker so Barton can hear, because we're both so damn curious that we can't wait. That photo on FaceBook that Margot posted– from a cafe. What *was* that guy doing to your hand? It looked like minor surgery – and wasn't he the one we met at the food fair, and you said he always mocks you? It's only a side view but it does look like him. About fifteen people have commented already and everyone's having a theory. We think they're excited seeing you with a new man.'

'He never did intend to mock me,' said Sofia, deciding to tackle the simplest question first. 'It was just his eyebrows.'

She heard Barton's bark of laughter and Sian said, 'What? His eyebrows? Have you been drinking? You sound very unlike yourself.'

'Don't be silly, of course I haven't been drinking

at eight in the morning. But he's very dark haired, and his eyebrows are a straight and kind of angle up at the outer corners and it makes him look devilish, or sarcastic if you like. So, I always took what he said as sarcasm. But I was wrong.'

There was a longish pause at the other end and Sofia, now sitting up, waited patiently. She knew her explanation wasn't enough to satisfy them, but she wasn't going to rush into anything, not with these two who knew her very well indeed and would never let her forget it if she revealed too much.

'OK,' said Barton finally, and she could tell he was trying not to laugh. 'I think we get that. I can't precisely picture his eyebrows, but I'll take your word for it. Why were you there with him in the first place, if you didn't like him and what was going on with the medical procedure?'

'He just happened to be there when I had a little accident! Don't get so damn excited, it was a coincidence.' She should be used to this by now, the endless quest of some of her friends to find a boyfriend for her, or even a casual date. None of them believed her when she shrugged it off and said it wasn't important, that she was perfectly happy on her own.

'Yeah, OK – but what was he doing to your

hand, you can see he's putting some kind of dressing on it,' said Sian impatiently. 'What happened?'

Five minutes later she put the phone down and got out of bed, hoping she had satisfied them that it was a chance, but lucky meeting – she with her dislocated finger and someone right there with extensive first aid knowledge. It wasn't until she was putting the plastic bag over her hand, ready to get into the shower, that she realised that she never asked where they saw the photo. Either Instagram or FaceBook, she thought, but maybe Twitter. Margot might be on Twitter, but Sofia wasn't. Pulling the bag off her hand again, she went back to the bedroom and sat on the bed to investigate.

And there on her FaceBook newsfeed was the post in question; the photo Margot had taken through the window, and though she had posted it with no text at all, Sofia's name was mentioned in several comments. She read the first few with a feeling of slight unreality. That kind of attention had never been directed at her before, and it made her cringe to feel so exposed to the eyes of the world. The photo was slightly unclear due to the reflection in the window, but Paul's profile and her own were clearly visible as were the supplies he had put on the table. The price you pay when you sit right inside a window, she thought, you're on public display. I didn't even notice anyone stopping to take a photo, but I wasn't really in a state to take much notice of anything. And why didn't Margot just come in and ask what had happened instead of posting it on social media? What a crazy world!

At lunchtime the sun was warm enough to sit on the little recessed balcony off her sitting room and read with a cup of coffee. When she first considered buying the apartment, the balcony was one of the things that attracted her. The idea that you could sit outside in Wellington, sheltered from the prevailing wind, was a feature that ranked high on the list of what was desirable. Sofia loved reading in the sun, experiencing that wonderful feeling of skin warmed by the sun, even if through clothing. The balcony was tiny with just enough room for a little table and two chairs, but because the glass door opened to the full width of it by folding inwards like a concertina, it felt as if the whole room opened up.

When her phone buzzed in the kitchen, she nearly ignored it, but the urge that always made her check who it was, drove her to get up. She had recently discussed this with Helen, who had said, 'I totally get it, I'm like it too, I can't ignore my phone, it's like I'm scared I'll miss something important and lifechanging. And I *do* know that not very long ago, people could only answer a phone call when they were at home and it obviously didn't ruin their lives, but we've been re-programmed, haven't we?'

And Sofia had laughed and agreed that the fear that we might miss out on something was now hard-wired in our brains. 'And it only took twenty-odd years to achieve that once we had cell phones – I bet technology is changing us faster than evolution ever did.'

So now she picked up the phone from the kitchen bench and took the call from Patsy, nearly regretting that she had un-blocked her only a few days ago.

'Well, well!' said her mother in the voice that usually meant some disapproving or sarcastic comment was heading her way. 'And who is that handsome profile tending to your hand? Have you finally got a man in your life again?'

'The most fortunate thing!' said Sofia casually, knowing that making light of things without hesitation was the key to keeping Patsy under control. 'I dislocated my finger by getting it caught in the doorhandle going in at that café, and as luck would have it a colleague was standing just inside, and he used to be a paramedic, so he knew just what to do.'

'But how did he get all the stuff I can see on the table?'

Patsy sounds accusing more often than anyone else I know, thought Sofia, it's as if she always suspects you of holding something back or lying. 'They lent him their first aid kit from the kitchen,' she said patiently. 'It didn't need much specialised stuff once the finger was back in place. Very painful, though – far worse than I would have expected.'

When they finished the conversation, Sofia sat down and responded to various comments under that irritating FaceBook post, explaining what had happened in the hope of taking the heat out of the situation. It might not work; her friends were always trying to set her up with dates and found it hard to grasp that she was perfectly happy as she was. Her whatever-it-was, friendship or relationship with Paul was slightly confusing and undefined, and she was not ready to discuss it, however well-meaning her friends were.

Chapter 16

While walking into the wind down Taranaki Street to meet Helen for Sunday morning coffee at Enigma, Sofia thought of the FaceBook post and what it had started, things that Margot had presumably not even considered when she posted it: intense and embarrassing interest from friends and relatives, and Sofia's private life invaded. I must bring it up with Margot, she thought, I have to tell her to be careful what she puts on social media, but without making her mad – she's so quick to get defensive about anything I say. Perhaps I say it wrong, perhaps I need a special technique to talk to Margot? I'll discuss it with Helen first, she's closer to Margot than I am.

Bringing it up with Helen became an obsolete notion when they sat down after placing their orders.

'What *was* going on in that café, Sofe? I know that guy - well, I don't actually *know* him, but I've met him. He's gorgeous – how on earth did you get together with him?'

Before she replied, Sofia studied the animated face of her best friend, the fast-talking woman, whose brain sometimes seemed to have no filter and who frequently said what others might think but would never say out loud. Helen clearly had no idea that what she had said could be taken as insulting, her green eyes were shining with curiosity, and she was smiling widely.

'I know I'm not as beautiful as you are,' said Sofia, pretending to be meek. 'But do you really have to be so blunt about my appearance?'

Helen's expression slowly morphed from excitement to confusion and finally to hilarity. 'Oh, for God's sake, darling! Of course, I didn't mean it like that, I'd never say anything so unkind to you, would I? You're just so cute in your own serious way, big brown eyes and all. I've always wished I could have a mouth like yours.'

She *would* say anything! thought Sofia. She's great at keeping secrets, but her instant reactions are sometimes off the scale of what's acceptable, but all she said was, 'I'm just kidding, Helen. I'll explain about the first aid session, and you can explain what on earth you mean about my mouth – but *not* before we've got out coffee.'

'So!' said Helen a few minutes later, pushed her plate with a doughnut to one side and leaned her elbows on the table. 'How do you know what's-his-name, the gorgeous guy? I can't remember his name, Paul something, I think. And what was he doing?'

'You obviously haven't been on FaceBook since I posted the explanation - it was pure coincidence,' said Sofia and tried to look casual. 'I've met him in court, we were once on opposite sides of a case ages ago, but I don't really know him. But I dislocated my little finger when it got caught in the doorhandle when I was going into that café, and he was already there, standing just inside the door. He used to be a paramedic, and he saw what happened, so he took over and reverted to his previous profession.'

'There's something about him,' said Helen. 'I think I heard something a year or two ago – some tragedy or accident or something, but I can't remember the details. Or it might have been that employment law guy, you know the one who rides a bike with his briefcase in a basket on the front, like old ladies used to – those two have the same kind of dark, brooding look.'

'Do you categorise men according to their looks?' asked Sofia, who often found that her conversations with Helen made her laugh more than talking to anyone else did. Teasing her was so rewarding. 'Like "he's one of the dark-haired hunks" or "one of the tall, slim blond boys" – or is it based on how sexy they are?'

Helen took a bite of her doughnut and said with her mouth full, 'Don't be silly! Of course, I don't – I just kind of link things in my mind sometimes for some reason. Like whenever I see that woman who's the deputy leader of the Nation Party on TV, I immediately think of Boofhead.'

She noticed the look on Sofia's face and laughed. 'Sorry, you haven't met him. Boofhead is my brother's dog – they've got exactly the same jawline, but he drools a lot, which what's-her-name doesn't do, or at least I hope she doesn't.'

When they finished laughing, Helen said with some hesitation, not an emotion Sofia usually associated with her, 'You mustn't tell anyone, but I'm writing a crime novel. I've no idea if it's going to be any good. I've only just started it, or I don't know if I'll ever finish it, but I'd like you to read it when I've got a bit further.'

This was nearly as surprising as the comment about Boofhead. 'I'd love to read it - what an amazing thing to do! What got you into this? You've never said you wanted to write before.'

'Oh, I don't want to write - it's just that I thought of a brilliant way to kill someone so nobody would ever find the body,' said Helen, her eyes gleaming with enthusiasm. 'And I don't think anyone's done it before, with grain, yes, maybe – but not flour. So, I thought I'd stake a claim to the idea by writing a book – you know, kind of timestamp it.'

'Please explain! I'm baffled,' said Sofia. 'And would you just this once start at the beginning, so I understand what you're talking about. You often leave me floundering in your wake, and then a few days later the penny drops, and I get what you meant.'

'You know how factories that make bread and things and use lots of flour have silos, and then big trucks that look like tanker trucks come and pump tons of flour into them? You didn't? Well, it's true, that's how they store all the flour. They need huge quantities of course, and those silos can take up to forty tons – I've looked into this. And there's a round lid, on the top and a ladder up the side, so the tanker guy climbs up and attaches a big, fat duct from the truck and then he pumps the flour into the silo.'

Helen drank some of her coffee and picked up the doughnut, but she didn't take a bite, she just gesticulated with it, scattering icing sugar over the table. 'And here's another amazing thing – they have to earth the duct, because the friction of the flour racing through can cause static electricity to build up and cause a spark so the flour explodes. It could blow the whole thing up – truck, silo, driver – the lot. Isn't it interesting?'

She took a bite finally and put the doughnut down, drank some more coffee and continued. 'Anyway, my idea is that you kill someone, or perhaps you just drug them so they're helpless, and then you drag them up the ladder, undo the lid on the top of the silo and drop the body in, headfirst, of course! Provided they're not too fat, so they fit through the hole. What do you think about that?'

Sofia picked up Helen's half doughnut, took a bite and chewed while she pictured the scene in her mind before she replied. 'It sounds very effective - I suppose the body would disappear down into the flour, like a diver into water and not be visible from that manhole or whatever you call it? And if the person wasn't dead already, they would inhale flour and suffocate. My God, Helen, this is brilliant! But wouldn't the body appear at the bottom eventually, kind of mummified from being in all that dry flour? It might block the place they get the flour out of.'

'Can I have my doughnut back, please? Or should I just get another one?'

'Sorry! Here you are, I just had to have one bite,'

said Sofia and laughed. 'Just like at primary school when we were always sharing our lunches.'

Helen smiled. 'I remember the nutbars your mum used to put in your box, lovely! But to get back to the flour silo, there's another round opening down near the bottom, and another big duct that the flour flows through to the factory. So, I think the body could remain there for a long time, at the very bottom, maybe forever. I'm working on the theory that the bread or whatever they make wouldn't taste funny, though, but how would they completely empty the silo to check anyway?'

They sat in silence for a few moments, thinking of that body head down in tons of flour, gone without a trace to possibly never be found.

'It's brilliant!' said Sofia again. 'Let me know when you're doing it, and provided it's not somebody I'm fond of, I'll come and help you haul the body up the ladder.'

H alf an hour later, with another cup of coffee each, Sofia said with no particular emphasis, knowing the answer might be one word or a torrent, 'And how is Oscar? How's the theatrical production going?'

Oscar and Helen had lived together for four or five years, and Helen used to tell people he was commitment reluctant. She would say things like, 'I proposed to Oscar the other day, but he's still commitment reluctant, so no joy this time.'

Once, after a few drinks, she confessed to Sofia that she proposed to him over breakfast on the first Sunday of every month.

'Oscar?' she said now, looking surprised, as if she hadn't heard the name mentioned for a long time.

'He's at home recovering, probably still in shock. I doubt he'll go anywhere today.'

'What happened? Did he have an accident surfing?' Oscar was known to pick the spots on the Wellington south coast where the gales hit with the most force and risk life and limb on his surfboard, but Helen just smiled.

'No, but his world view got a bit of a shake-up last night. And if I tell you the story, you must promise not to mention it – I don't want the poor guy to be embarrassed, but I know you'll appreciate it. So, here's what happened. We were talking about a pension fund thing we're involved with, and I said, maybe we should combine our investments and get into a higher interest bracket, and he said, "oh no, you never know what will happen in the future, I don't think couples should combine their pension investments" which is exactly what I expected.' She grinned. 'I would probably have said the same thing, so I said, "I agree, easy come, easy go" – and he asked what I meant.'

Sofia can think of several things to say but picks the one that seems to be expected. 'What *did* you mean?'

'I could have meant the money, or us, our relationship. But I said, "oh, nothing in particular, it just popped out by mistake" and then he asked if I was thinking of breaking up and the whole thing get more and more intense, but I refused to satisfy him, and I never said that of course I wouldn't ever leave him, I just left him dangling. It sucked the juice right out of him, he couldn't get over it - that I said something along the lines of what *he* always says when I propose to him. And then this morning I didn't propose as I usually do over breakfast on the first Sunday of the month.'

Sofia laughed so hard she got tears in her eyes and Helen joined in, while the elderly couple at the next table stared disapprovingly at them as if they had broken some unwritten rule of café behaviour. 'You're so funny, but that was evil! Please let me know what happens next. Perhaps he'll be waiting when you get back, on his knees in the hall, ready to propose.'

'Ha!' said Helen, 'not him! But it was fun changing the agenda a bit and time will tell, as my mum always says, no point in trying to guess how this will end.'

Sofia knew the prospect of breaking up with Oscar would also break Helen's heart, but she admired her cool approach; how she had managed to turn a situation around, remove herself from the centre of the potential vortex, crack a joke or wait.

They stood talking for a few more minutes

outside the café, and Sofia remembered that she was going to ask Helen to talk to Margot.

'It's not that she doesn't understand about privacy, I don't think,' she said. 'It was probably more unthinking, and I'm sure she wouldn't tell any secrets about other people's affairs or whatever, but she could cause quite a bit of bother by doing what she did. She clearly didn't know who the guy bandaging my hand was – what if he'd been married or in a tricky relationship and someone thought we were on a date? It's just bad manner so post stuff like that, careless.'

'Is he married?' asked Helen, looking searchingly at Sofia.

'I don't know if he is or isn't – that's not the point. So, can you please talk to Margot some time, just casually? You'll do it so much better than I would. If I do it, she'll get upset and defensive and then it will turn into a nightmare. She always thinks I'm lecturing her or something, once she said I make her feel that she's five years old. Or maybe she said that I think she's five years old.'

No more than a couple of minutes after parting, Helen appeared beside Sofia and caught hold of her arm. 'I forgot,' she panted. 'I said I'd tell you about your mouth.'

Sofia burst out laughing at this unexpected

reappearance and said, 'Are you serious? You ran after me to tell me about my mouth? Helen, I do love you, but sometimes I think you're crazy.'

'Oh, probably – but listen, I'd like you to know, because sometimes I get the feeling you've got no idea how cute you are. So, here goes – your mouth is, according to Oscar, very "kissable" which I gather means that men look at your mouth and whether they love you or lust after you - or not, they just feel they want to kiss you.'

Sofia could think of nothing to say, her mind was swirling with embarrassment and surprise. She stared at Helen, who seemed to be waiting for an answer.

'Aren't you flattered? I would be! I've got a mouth that men only want to kiss if they are falling in love with me or they're drunk and would kiss a pig.'

Gathering her composure like a protective cloak around her, Sofia said calmly, 'Oh, it's very flattering – I never knew that, never thought of it. But what concerns me now, is how I'll feel next time I meet Oscar!'

'Oh, for God's sake, don't even think about it – he frequently comments on women, and he won't have a clue I told you. You know you can trust me on this – haven't we been keeping each other's secrets since we were ten?'

And that was true, thought Sofia as she continued

on her way, I can trust her and that might be the most surprising thing about her and something a lot of people wouldn't know; she is not only the most loyal friend I have, and she's also the most trustworthy.

Chapter 18

Tuesday was not a court day and Sofia was typing notes into a Word document, when Clare put her head around the door and said, 'Mr Somerville's son is on the phone. Do you want to talk to him or are you concentrating?'

'I'll talk to him, thanks,' she said and saved the paragraph she had just added to her notes.

'I just have to tell you what happened,' said the man who introduced himself as Stanley. 'Dad and I went and picked up that motor home from the fraudster and Dad fell in love with it on sight, and now he says he's going to keep it! He went inside and couldn't believe his eyes, and to be honest neither could I, it's like a little flat with a proper bedroom at the far end. And it's got everything you could wish for – modern appliances, toilet and shower, TV – the lot! All you have to do is plug it in to charge now and then. So, he turned to me with this huge grin and asked if it was legal to live in thing like that permanently, and if it was, he wanted to live in it.'

'How funny!' said Sofia and tried to imagine Mr Somerville driving a gigantic house-bus when he seemed nearly too wobbly to drive a car safely. 'Is he safe to drive it, do you think? And where would he keep it? Surely not at that flat he lives in?'

'Oh, no he's not driving it anywhere. I'm going to take it to his widowed sister's place and he's going to park it beside her house. She says she'd love the company – she's at least ten years younger than him so she'll be able to keep a bit of an eye on him. I just called the guy in New Plymouth and thanked him for his kind offer and told him the story and said he doesn't need to buy it back after all. So, I wanted to thank you, too, because this is a great result. And dad will sell his flat and still have some savings – quite a lot, actually, more than he would have got by selling the motorhome.'

'Another good ending,' said Sofia and held out their celebration box of chocolates, and Clare looked up from her computer, looked at the box in Sofia's hand

and said, 'What are we celebrating? Obviously, something Mr Somerville's son told you.'

Sofia pulled over Clare's visitor's chair and sat down with the box on the desk between them. 'A lovely ending, just wait till you hear it – particularly since I had doubts about that case being winnable at all. Well, not the fraud part, of course, but that the poor old chap would get his savings back.'

'I'll add it to his notes right away,' said Clare when she had finished the story and took another foil wrapped chocolate out of the box. 'Do you think we're the only team who do this? Add the extra bits to the client notes when something particularly good happens as a result? I don't think anybody else in this firm does it, but I have a feeling Grant might after he heard about our last happy outcome notes. I've never heard of the idea before, and this is the third law firm I've worked for – I think you're unique in the legal world.'

'I just like to think that those things aren't forgotten. Sometimes we see people who're devastated by something that's been done to them, or who have been injured and not got any justice, but this kind of thing makes up for it.'

When Sofia got a text from Margot later that morning asking if they could meet "somewhere convenient to you" at lunchtime that day, she took for granted that Helen had already said something to her about the FaceBook photo. Margot had never asked to meet her before and having lunch with her was not an inviting prospect. Ever since they had first met through a book club a couple of years ago, Margot seemed to have suspected Sofia of being dismissive. Sofia didn't know quite what it was, and that comment about 'you think I'm a five-year old' was only one aspect of it. Once or twice after meeting Margot in a social context with Helen or at the monthly book club evening, she had tried to analyse what it could be that had tainted what Margot thought of her. She knew, though, that to turn down the offer of meeting for lunch would only make matters worse, so she replied and said "Yes, let's" and asked what time Margot took her lunch hour.

Chapter 19

As Sofia walked towards Neo Café, which Margot had suggested, she tried to imagine the best way to react when Margot brought up the issue of the photo, as she was certain to do. She could pretend it didn't matter, or she could say that perhaps it had been a bit embarrassing, but however she put it she knew it would only inflate Margot's sense of perceived inferiority. The one thing she couldn't do was say it didn't matter. Damn it, she thought, I wish I didn't feel obliged to meet her face to face over this! I'll get it wrong whatever I say, as I always seem to with her.

Sofia went inside to wait by the door rather than stand outside in the typical Wellington wind that always seemed to funnel up Willis Street and get colder as it went, but as she looked around, she saw

Margot waving from a table and pointing at the order number stick in front of her.

'That wind!' said Sofia when she had ordered. She hung her jacket on the back of the chair opposite Margot and sat down. 'How are you? You weren't at book club last time.'

'I had a miscarriage – a messy one,' said Margot bluntly, and Sofia reached across and curled her fingers around Margot's hand, instantly filled with pity, because she could see the distress the other woman felt. She had tried to conceal it by being matter of fact, but her eyes betrayed her. 'I'm so sorry - that must have been awful! I didn't know you were pregnant.'

'I'm one of those strange women, whose bodies hide the baby.' She hesitated for a moment. 'I was just up to five months, and it got a bit traumatic because they couldn't stop the bleeding.'

She pulled her hand away from Sofia's when a waitress arrived with their orders. 'It's kind of you to ...' and then her voice tapered off, as if she didn't know how to finish the sentence.

'I've never been pregnant,' said Sofia, trying to fill the gap without seeming callous or as if she was trying to make light of what Margot had told her. She looked down at her hand stirring sugar into her coffee and made a snap decision to share something she never talked about. 'I was in a two-year relationship a few years ago, but I had a feeling nearly from the start that it might not work out in the long term. For some personal reason he didn't want me to take the pill, said he wouldn't mind starting a family if I happened to get pregnant, but I continued to take the pill without telling him – and he never found out. And it turned out to be a very lucky decision.'

In the back of her mind, she wondered why she brought this up, the lead-up to a distressing chapter in her life that she would rather forget, but something about Margot's face when she mentioned her miscarriage had triggered it.

'Why didn't it work out?' Margot was looking straight into her eyes now, as if their rather sketchy and slightly untrusting relationship had turned into a new one that demanded honesty and the right to ask uncomfortable questions.

'I don't know what it was at the start, just some kind of vibe that I couldn't even explain to myself. Afterwards I tried to identify where that feeling came from, why I continued to take the pill. It must have had something to do with the idea that if I had a baby I'd be locked into that relationship – I really can't say, it wasn't a conscious thought. So, I kept the pills in my desk drawer at work because I was even worried he would start looking through my things, he was obsessed with knowing everything, checking I had no secrets. And still I stayed with him – incomprehensible now.'

She paused and wondered if she should continue, if it would seem selfish to go and on a about herself and if she would regret it later. But she could sense that it had diverted Margot and that she was genuinely interested. 'But over time he became controlling, more and more so, on every level you can imagine. And I broke it off.'

On an impulse she interrupted Margot, who was just bout to speak. 'Helen picked it up right off before I could see for myself what he was like. She told me she was worried about how passive aggressive he was, long before I saw it for what it was - and I didn't quite believe her, so I stayed a bit too long. Longer than was good for my mental health. It made me doubt my ability to evaluate people and it made me *very* distrustful of men, particularly good-looking ones.'

At the end of an hour, Sofia felt that the lunch had been an eye-opener and she could tell that Margot was as surprised as she was herself. To have known someone for a couple of years and never made a connection seemed very odd, now that they had found such a lot to talk about and been able to sympathise about traumatic events. Saying goodbye outside in the chilly wind, Margot turned up her coat collar and said, 'Oh, I totally forgot why I asked you to meet me! I wanted to apologise for that photo of you I posted on FaceBook – I had no idea it would generate such a storm of comments! I was sorry when I discovered the attention it was getting, but it had already spread when I went to delete it - too many people we both know had shared it.'

'Never mind,' said Sofia casually, as if she had never been in the least worried. 'It was such a strange little event, a quiet little drama – I'll fill you in next time we have lunch, but now I must run. I have a client meeting in ten minutes.'

Though she was in a hurry, she stopped in a sheltered doorway and texted Helen. 'Pls don't say anything to Margot abut FB photo, she has apologised.' Then she ran the rest of the way with the phone still in her hand and made it back just in time.

Late that evening, on a whim, Sofia decided to call Storm, because the dinner at Logan Brown had been so full-on and noisy with people talking across each other and the teenagers demanding explanations about old stories they had never heard before, that she hadn't got a chance to have a proper conversation with Storm.

'Is something wrong?' he said. 'It's not something bad is it, like illness or death?'

'Nothing like that! I just felt after the birthday dinner that we never got to talk properly and then you were all so busy and I had to go to work and so on. Just a catch-up if you have time.'

'Fine,' said Storm and she heard him open the fridge and started laughing. 'I bet you're getting a beer out to keep you going while we talk?'

'Yep – I haven't got the kids this week, so there's nobody to nag at me about my waistline if I have a beer before dinner. Bet you have a glass of wine beside you – an after-dinner one at your end, I suppose. Sometimes I forget the time difference and call mum when it's ten o'clock in the evening here and wake her up in the middle of the night.'

They talk about Christina and Gregory and how nice they are, halfway to adulthood and still act as if they quite like adults.

'They're not too bad, not like some,' said Storm. 'Some of my friends have kids who act as if their parents are their worst enemies – telling them they're useless and being really dismissive, and then they turn around and ask to use their mum's car to drive to the fast-food place a few hundred meters down the road – true! I heard that story yesterday from a mate.'

'Entitlement syndrome,' said Sofia. 'Which I take to mean that they have unrealistic expectations of what's due to them. My friends mostly don't have kids old enough to talk about this, but I read about it. Hey, isn't it great that Summer's got a girlfriend, finally some action?'

'Did mum tell you they're getting married? We're coming over for the wedding late January, I've forgotten the date. Will you be there?'

Sofia laughed. 'If I get invited, I will. Where is it?'

'I just got an email from her a couple of days ago - the ceremony is going to be in the Dunedin botanical garden and then a reception at the house – they're going to live in Summer's house because it's nicer than what's-her-name's place.'

'Now – I must tell you about that court case you helped me with by asking questions on TradeMe, and what happened afterwards, a great result all round.'

When she put down the phone they had talked for nearly an hour. She put her glass in the dishwasher and went to bed with Ender's Game.

Chapter 20

The text from Sian had arrived on Wednesday morning while Sofia was in the shower, and which she discovered when she picked up her phone while waiting for the toaster to pop.

"Dinner at our place tonight? Barton wants to try a new recipe and it's for eight pp! Drinks at 7, dinner whenever the food is ready."

Sofia replied, "Yes thanks, lovely!" and wondered if eight for dinner included the triplets, or if she had invited six guests. Sometimes Sian tried to set her up with someone; once or twice it had been embarrassingly blatant, but a couple of mildly enjoyable dates had resulted, though not anything she wanted to take further. Once Barton had said, pretending he was joking, but really trying to find out what sat behind her reluctance to get even close to becoming serious about someone, 'Are you waiting for the prince to come, Sofia?'

'I'm just very picky,' she had said and laughed, not wanting to discuss it, because the answer was that after her experience with a controlling man, she had lost confidence in her ability to recognise the warning signs, and now she was very cautious. She had only got to know Sian and Barton after leaving that disastrous relationship, and she had never told them any details. On some occasions when someone asked if she had a man in her life, she would say that casual dating was so much simpler, nobody to accommodate, nobody who would resent being told she had to work late. Once or twice, she had told a well-meaning woman friend that she couldn't be bothered getting into something even half-serious, when a year down the track she might meet someone whom she really and truly loved, with no doubts, no hesitation.

Next a text from Paul: "Would you like to have dinner on Friday at Fujiyama? Or somewhere else if you don't like Japanese food."

Sofia replied: "Sounds great - about seven? I can book, I walk past on my way home.'

She had no sooner settled down to her breakfast when another text arrived from Sian: "Please don't bring chocolates!"

Sofia had no idea what this meant, or why Sian thought she might bring chocolates, which as far as she could recall she had never done, but she fired off an "OK" and turned her attention back to her toast and the Guardian app on her phone.

Later that morning her phone signalled a call just as she was showing clients out of her office, and she ignored it until they had said their goodbyes, expecting the caller to have hung up before she got back to her desk, but no, Marcus had not hung up.

'You're very patient,' she said. 'Is it important or haven't you got anyone to talk to?'

'I'm standing beside a car in a suburb waiting for a guy to come out of his house. I need to serve a summons and he's been very elusive, but I think I'll get him this time. The bailiff guy I usually get to do these jobs for me got so sick of trying and failing that I set out early and watched his house one morning. So now I know which car is his and I'm standing right by the passenger door pretending to look at something on my phone, but I'm just waiting and talking to you to pass the time. I've got my strategy planned – when he goes around to unlock the driver's door and get in, I'll open the passenger door, slide in and film myself serving the papers. So, if I suddenly stop talking you'll know why.'

'Is that it? You called because you're bored? How long have you been there?'

'About fifteen minutes – but it's OK, he can't see me until he comes out on the street. I just checked our group page on FaceBook – have you seen the comments?'

'What comments? Has something happened?'

'You're the hot topic, Sofe – I've never seen so many comments, go and have a look. I think everyone in the group has commented. Ah, here comes the elusive Mr Martin now. Talk later!'

What she saw, when she checked the Ridiculous Phrase page on FaceBook, was nearly overwhelming. Someone in the group had seen the photo Margot took trough the café window and shared it, and the comments from the group would have been hilarious if they had been about someone else; suggestions about amputations, a ring that was stuck, a café tattooist and some more personal. Without acknowledging them in any way she went further back to her own post about which book her winning phrase had come from and now she laughed. Everyone in the group had commented there too, and then commented on each other's comments. Long streams of opinions and jokes and emojis, all based on their assumption that the woman they had known since they started their law studies had either undergone a personality transplant, had suffered a head injury or was being impersonated by a romantic girl of sixteen.

"Romantic historical novels!!! The most studious and serious girl in our year? Who would have thought?" Followed by a I'm-laughing-until-I-cry emoji from Rory, who once managed to get Sofia into bed at his flat after a party, and then fell instantly asleep before anything took place. She remembered looking at him still sound asleep the next morning when she quietly got dressed and tip-toed out the front door and went home. She had thought it might be fun to have sex with Rory, who was very handsome as well as kind and clever, but fate and alcohol had other plans.

She posted only one comment of her own: "Still the same person, no hidden secrets — you lot just didn't dig deep enough!" followed by a laughing face emoji.

Chapter 21

Arriving at Sian and Barton's house she noticed nothing unusual until she went in through the half-open front door and saw the balloons and the streamers. She stopped dead and thought hard, but nothing came to mind; no birthdays, no hints about potential new jobs and definitely not another baby.

'Here she is!' Sian's voice was louder than usual, her face was flushed, and Sofia thought she looked like she usually did after three drinks, not at the start of an evening. 'Great! Now we're all here.'

She yelled in the direction of the kitchen. 'Barton! Sofia's here!' Then she turned to her brother, 'Patrick, would you please pour her a glass of bubbly?'

'What's going on?' said Sofia with a glass of champagne in her hand. 'This is so unexpected –

mid-week and instant action. Can't be just that Barton is experimenting with new food, surely? I know he's a culinary wonder, but this?'

Sian's older brother Patrick, twice divorced and one of the men Sian had tried to get Sofia hooked up with, laughed and shook his head. 'Believe it or not, they've refused to tell us a thing. Sian's so excited she's about to burst into flames. I can't even guess.'

Sofia looked around the room and counted heads. The triplets were there, building something with Lego in the corner of the living room that was always covered in new constructions, and from where tiny sharp pieces somehow migrated across the room, unnoticed until you stepped on one with bare feet. By the window stood Barton's sister and her partner, whose name she couldn't remember, talking to a woman she had never seen before, fortyish with long dark hair in a ponytail.

'Who is the dark-haired woman talking to Penny? Your date?'

Patrick grinned, 'Well, you didn't want me, so I had to find someone else – it's my fiancé Veronica, I'll introduce you.'

'Listen,' said Sofia quietly, 'don't say it like that – about me or anyone else not wanting you and having to find someone else – not in front of Veronica, she might feel insulted. Like she's second choice or something. Oh, here comes Barton.'

'Don't worry!' said Patrick in a whisper. 'I told her I'd been out with you a couple of times, but I said I didn't really fancy you!'

Before Sofia had time to reply, Barton clinked his glass with a spoon and pulled Sian against his side with an arm over her shoulders. 'We're celebrating that we won some money on Lotto – not a fortune but enough to renovate the upstairs and put in another bathroom … *and* for Sian to do what she has wanted to do for about a hundred years, or at least ten, open a bookshop specialising in New Zealand authors.'

Everybody cheered and exclaimed and raised their glasses, and the triplets did their victory lap as Barton called it, the get-rid-of-some-excitement trick he had devised when they were three or four. The ran cheering and yelling from the living room, through the hall and the kitchen and reappeared through the door from the dining room. The house seemed to reverberate with noise, excited voices asking questions and the children setting out on a second lap through the house.

'Congratulations!' Sofia hugged Sian and thought how lovely this was, such good friends who both worked hard, never had much money, and who were always kind and hospitable. Nobody deserved it more or would use the money to better effect.

'When did you find out, was it in the last draw? Must have been – you're still so excited!'

'It was an old ticket, very old, one of those bonus ones! Barton found it in his wallet a few days ago, and it was only another two weeks before it would have been too late to claim the prize! Isn't it wonderful! Imagine finding it when it was too late – it doesn't bear thinking about! He called some help desk number and it's all done - the claim's been confirmed.'

'And the chocolate? I don't think I've ever brought chocolate to your place, so what was that about?'

'It's the children – the little devils found where I'd hidden three or four boxes of chocolates people have given us, mostly my mum who nearly always brings one when she comes for dinner. The kids ate the lot – in one afternoon! I discovered what they had done when Anneliese was sick just before dinner and it looked like liquid mud all over the bathroom floor! So, now I've said no chocolates in this house for three months – not a single one of any kind.'

'And your mum's been informed?'

Sian gave her an evil smile. 'Oh, yes! I put the kids on my phone with the speaker on and made them confess what they'd done and ask her themselves not bring any more chocolates.'

Sofia laughed. 'You're the perfect parent – well done!'

Much later, when Sian and Sofia were in the kitchen loading the dishwasher, Sofia nearly told Sian about her dinner date with Paul, but even as she was opening her mouth to speak, something made her pull back. It was too new and too uncertain, and if she mentioned it and then nothing came of the date, she would have to explain when Sian asked about it, as she was sure to do. So instead, she asked what Patrick's fiancé did and if she had been married before and had children, and the conversation took up the rest of their time in the kitchen.

In the Uber on the way home she turned the sound back up on her phone and saw a message from Marcus; three images of his face with bruising around the jawline on one side and a black eye: "Got him on video doing this! Painful, but worth it! Summons served."

Chapter 22

When Sofia entered the office on Thursday morning, she noticed that Bayden, their receptionist, gave her an amused look, and when Clare came to ask her something mid-morning, she had the same look on her face; intrigued and amused at the same time.

'OK,' said Sofia. 'What's going on here today? Have I missed something? Bayden looked at me as if I'm suddenly either interesting or funny, when he normally looks at me as if I'm somebody rather dull he has to be polite to. And now you come in with a funny look on your face. What's going on?'

Clare smiled and said evasively, 'But you know that Bayden only looks properly at men, he's gay for heaven's sake. And I'm sure he doesn't think you're dull - he just relegates you and me to the background. He's not one of those gay guys who have women as friends, I don't think.'

'So why did *you* look at me like that, then? Come on, Clare. I hope it's not some practical joke about to happen – I hate practical jokes.'

'It's just that FaceBook photo – someone saw it and it's been shown to everyone in the office this morning, and they're all intrigued. I know it's not brand new, but you know how it is. Posts from days ago arrive on someone's newsfeed as if they were new. Everything about the handsome Mr Strong is of interest to a lot of women – and obviously to some men too!' She laughed. 'And now they're all wondering if there's something going on between you two and how that happened. It's just that you never talk about dates or mention any men, or even show any interest, so the girls got a bit excited about it.'

'Really? Is that all it is? How ridiculous – tell them it was a chance meeting, and very lucky for me. He used to be a paramedic and he fixed my dislocated finger, that's all - he saw it happen, so he got the first aid kit from the kitchen and strapped my fingers up.'

And thankfully they won't know that I've seen him again, thought Sofia, imagine the excitement that would cause, not to mention that I'm having dinner with him tomorrow!

'OK, I'll dampen it down a bit,' said Clare, but the slightly amused look didn't leave her face. 'And you asked me to remind you about the staff meeting on Monday – you said there was something you might need to submit for the agenda. Let's hope the excitement about the FaceBook post has died down by then.'

Instead of commenting further, Sofia got up. 'I'm going to pop out and have a coffee and something to eat – it's kind of brunch time now and I didn't have breakfast. Do you want me to bring you something back?'

'A sandwich would be good – saves me going out at lunchtime. Anything that doesn't have egg in it.'

The café where Sofia usually went was surprisingly quiet and she took one of the magazines from the rack by the counter and retired to a booth. She was halfway through her toasted sandwich and an article about cycleways, when a couple came across the room and sat down on the other side of the little partition behind her. She glanced at them as they approached and thought the woman looked familiar, thought perhaps she worked for the law firm on the next floor down from her own office, but there was no sign of recognition, so she returned her attention to the article. A few minutes later she heard the woman mention Paul's name, so she put her magazine down and turned her head to eavesdrop on the conversation in the booth behind her.

I never realised he was an object of gossip, she thought, I've never heard anyone talking about him before, and just then the woman said, 'I don't know who that girl was either, but maybe he's got two on the go at the same time. He might be multi-dating, who knows?'

'I thought I recognised her profile,' said the man, 'but with the reflection in the glass I couldn't see her properly, so I might be wrong. And what do you mean by multi-dating? Is this a new expression your kids have taught you?'

'Pretty self-explanatory I think, my daughter uses it all the time. They say he's recently hooked up with some tall, blond woman, very elegant. Our admin manager saw them meeting in a bar a couple of weeks ago and said they seemed very affectionate. The girl in that photo obviously isn't her, she's got dark hair and she didn't look tall.'

Sofia got up, leaving half her lunch, and set out to get a sandwich for Clare from the place further down the block, keen to get away before she was recognised, increasingly tired of the attention. She considered cancelling her dinner date with Paul, reluctant to get involved with someone who was obviously an object of interest and gossip, and who might well be dating multiple women. The complications that could arise from going out with a man like that were definitely not her scene. But for the first time in her life, she ignored her own common-sense warning and didn't cancel the date; she wanted to see him again, talk to him and feel that lovely warm strength directed at herself. I'll just have to be careful not to fall in love with him, she told herself as she headed back to the office with Clare's ham sandwich and a brownie in a bag. If he's already involved with someone, I'll just quietly and discretely lust after him and enjoy his company. I can always stop seeing him if I feel I'm in the danger zone.

Chapter 23

Sofia locked her door, checked the time on her phone and wondered if being punctual would make her seem too keen; the Fujiyama was only two blocks from her apartment, and she had ten minutes to get there.

She had been carrying on an internal dialogue all day, telling herself off for exposing herself to the risk of falling in love with a man, who was already involved with someone else, but seeing him again for what was, after all, just a casual dinner between two friends, seemed harmless, and she did want to see him again. But even after telling herself to be realistic and to expect nothing more than friendship, she had still spent nearly an hour deciding what to wear. After alternating between dressing in very casual clothes that she felt made her nearly unnoticeable and things that were more attention-seeking and made her feel special, she had finally opted for her grey jeans and her new tight-fitting sky-blue T-shirt under a black jacket. 'I know, I know!' she said aloud, when she studied her reflection in the full-length mirror on the wardrobe door. 'But there's nothing wrong with wanting to look your best, is there? And I don't often dress to show off my figure, this is as much for my self-confidence as it is for his benefit'

As she approached the restaurant, still thinking that maybe she should walk around the block so as not to arrive too early, she spotted Paul coming from the opposite direction and felt a smile break out. He got there first and stood holding the door open, and she walked in ahead of him saying over her shoulder, 'Watch your fingers!' and heard him chuckle behind her.

'How *is* the finger?' he asked when they were seated, and she held out her hand towards him. 'I think it's back to normal – more or less. I haven't had my little finger strapped to the ring finger for two days now.'

He took her hand and gently bent her little finger and that strange feeling of warmth once again flowed up her arm.

'Seems OK,' he said, and she pulled her hand

back, though she would have liked to leave it where it was, held in one of his. Watch it, girl, she silently admonished herself, don't show your feelings and ruin this friendship or get entangled in something silly. She was very aware that the little signals of interest and the knuckle kiss might just be affectionate friendliness, and she would rather have him as a friend than embarrass them both and have to cut the relationship off.

Halfway through the meal, he put his chopsticks down and wiped his forehead, and for a moment his eyes closed.

'Are you alright? You look very hot,' she said and suppressed the urge to reach out to touch him. He opened his eyes and smiled, but the smile looked forced. 'I think I'm coming down with something, but let's not worry about it right now.'

She studied him whenever he looked away or down at his plate and noticed how high his colour was and how beads of perspiration kept forming on his forehead, but she hesitated to ask again. Then suddenly he said, 'I think I need to get home – sorry!' He got to his feet, swayed as if he was about to fall and put a hand on the back of his chair to steady himself. Sofia decided that politeness and caution were no longer on the agenda. Quickly she rose, took a couple of steps closer and said, 'Please sit down

again while I go and pay. Like you said to me once –
you look like you're going to fall over.'

Much to her surprise he did sit down, and when
she glanced back from the desk where she was
waiting to pay, he was leaning his head in his hands
and looked ready to collapse.

'OK,' she said when she was back at their table,
'now you lean on me, I'm stronger than I look. I
don't want you to fall over.'

But once they were outside, things got worse.
Paul came to a stop and leaned against the wall as if
he had run out of steam, and when she reached up
to feel his forehead heat radiated out from him;
despite the cool evening air she felt it before she even
touched him. He's really ill, she thought, he's
running a temperature, and he's unsteady on his feet,
not a good sign.

'How did you get here? Where do you live?' If he
drove here, she thought, then I'll drive him home in
his car and then take a taxi back or whatever seems
most practical.

'Island Bay - bus,' he said and coughed. 'So, I
could have a drink.'

For a moment she hesitated, but he looked worse
now than he had in the restaurant, and she decided
he wasn't in a state to take himself home, and neither
was she happy about him being alone over the

weekend. What if he got worse and was too ill to call an ambulance?

'Come on,' said Sofia in her let's-not-have-any-nonsense voice that she occasionally used when she baby-sat Sian and Barton's triplets. 'Lean on me, it's only another block and a half.'

To her surprise he didn't protest, but their progress was slow and by the time they were in her apartment, he was buckling at the knees, and she was only just able to support him.

'Through here,' she said, and they managed to make it to her bedroom before he gave up. She could feel him drooping and managed to push him sideways onto the bed.

'Thank God he didn't land on the floor!' she said to herself and looked down at him, slumped half on and half off the bed, appearing to be asleep. 'You're in a terrible state, my friend.'

There was no sign he had heard her; his eyes remained closed and now he was shivering. Sofia spent a couple of minutes running options through her head, then she threw her jacket on the armchair by the window and started working. For the next half hour, she kept up a low-voiced running commentary in the hope that her words would penetrate whatever state he was in, in a faint or asleep, and provide some comfort. At least he'll know he's not alone, she thought, and maybe I'll be able to ask him some questions.

'Let's get your legs up on the bed and straighten you out a bit, and then I'll get your

shoes off. And I'll open up the other side of the bed like this and try to move you over, and then we'll get your gear off and tuck you in. Oh God, you're so heavy! That's *not* going to work. I wonder if I can roll you, no I can't, I'll just have to undress you first and then try to drag the covers out from under you and leave you on this side.'

She got his jacket off by labouriously half rolling him, first one way and then the other, then his shoes and socks and jeans. 'Don't panic,' she said, kneeling on the bed beside him. 'I'm just looking after *you* for a change, this is not an assault. And you'll need water, lots of it and maybe a cool, damp cloth would be good to wipe your face?'

Dragging the bedding from under him woke him up, and he stared up at her, confused and anxious looking. 'What's going on? What are you doing?'

She stopped the pulling and tugging, put her hand on his cheek and said in the calmest voice she could muster, 'I'm just putting you to bed, because you're very sick. Is there anyone at your place or do you live alone?'

'Alone – where are we?'

'You're at my place, just for now, don't worry. Any pets that need feeding at your place?'

'No.' His eyes closed again, and she bent over him and said loudly, 'Lift your bum a fraction so I can get this cover out from under you.'

A minute later he was tucked in, and she heaved a sigh of relief. 'Don't move! I'll be back in a moment.' Not that she was worried that he would try to get dressed and leave, but if he tried to stand and fell over, she knew she would never get him back on the bed again.

'Who would have thought he was so damn heavy?' she said to herself while she assembled her supplies, still speaking out loud. 'He is quite tall, and he's got broad shoulders, but still. Not that I've ever had to manhandle a helpless male body before, maybe they're all just heavier than they look.'

When she returned with a tray loaded with a bowl of iced water, a facecloth and a jug and a glass, his eyes were closed again, but they opened when he heard her moving things on her bedside table.

'I must go home,' he mumbled. 'Can't stay here - this is ridiculous.'

'No, it's not – you're far too sick to go home to an empty house. And you couldn't anyway, you'd fall over if you tried. You've already done that once, but luckily you managed to land half on the bed - you're far too heavy for me to lift off the floor. Now, raise your shoulders a bit so I can push another couple of pillows behind you, so you can drink.'

'Enough,' he said after one glass, and she took the opportunity to get the thermometer out of her pocket and stick it in his mouth. 'Don't talk.' When the little beep announced it was ready, she turned on the bedside light and gasped.

'Your temp is over thirty-nine – should I call an ambulance?'

'Shit no! Don't do that! I'm sure it's just flu or something.' His voice was raspy and sounded painful. 'I'll be able to tell if it gets to my lungs.' His eyes closed again, and she was left standing beside the bed listening to his rapid breathing, feeling helpless and very worried.

'Now I'll get myself organised,' she said out loud, because she realised that speaking rather than just thinking seemed to make things clearer, and it was for both their benefit.

'I'll get my laptop and a cup of coffee and set myself up in the armchair by the window, so I can watch him. I'll turn that light off and just have the one on the other side of the bed on, and I'll turn the ceiling light off.'

She picked up his clothes from where she had thrown them on the floor, put them in a neat pile on the floor by the wardrobe, pushed his shoes under the bed and went to organise her own supplies.

'Now it's too dark,' she said when she got back and off-loaded her things on the table beside the little blue armchair. 'What have I got that would just throw a little light at this end? Not the light from the coffee table, it takes up to much room, I need something small and dim. Oh, I know, I'll find that string of little bud-lights I had on the balcony last Christmas.'

Before long Sofia's bedroom had been reorganised into a combined workstation-cum-sickroom and she was sitting on the edge of the bed, wiping Paul's face with the cold, wet facecloth. He opened his eyes, but she could see he didn't really register who she was. He tried to push her hand away and she took hold of his wrist and bent over him.

'It's OK, Paul, don't worry,' she said softly, close to his face. 'You'll be all right; I'm looking after you. It's OK now, don't worry.' A steam of comforting words, a human voice speaking softly, to reassure him.

'Information is what I need,' she whispered to herself when he had settled down again. 'And who would have thought this little armchair, and the table would be so useful one day, I hardly ever sit here even though I love this little blue chair.'

She searched the Health Department website for flu information and heaved a sigh of relief at the concise bullet point list she found. After saving the link she sat thinking through what she had learnt, the length of time he would probably need care, the danger signals that she must look out for in case he developed complications like pneumonia and needed to be taken to hospital, and how long he would be infectious. 'But that doesn't matter,' she said aloud to herself. 'I've been all over him already, so if I'm going to get sick it's already too late. I've got to look after him and we'll deal with the consequences later.'

By two in the morning Paul was tossing and turning, and Sofia wiped him repeatedly with cold water, pulled the sheet off him and wiped his chest under his T-shirt, but his temperature still rose slowly. After a struggling to get his T-shirt off and nearly resorting to cutting it open, she sat down to consider what to do next, but she could think of nothing except simply carrying on doing what she was already doing

If this was purely viral with no bacterial infection to complicate it, as it seemed to be at the moment, then antibiotics would change nothing. Getting water into him was hard work and she felt awful about ordering him to drink, holding the glass to his mouth, and even contemplating pouring water right down his throat. She knew that getting enough fluids into him was vital, but she had never realised how hard this would be, when someone was only half-awake and resisting.

Worrying that she would fall asleep in the armchair and not notice if his condition changed, so she got into leggings and a sweatshirt and lay down on top of the duvet on the other side of the bed, listening to his panting breaths and planning how to deal with work. Then she realised she couldn't remember her diary entries for Monday, so she got up again to check online and found that most things scheduled for the coming week could be postponed or transferred to someone else in the firm. Thank God, I have nothing in court, she thought, because this has to take precedence over work. She sent an email to Clare asking her to tell the others that she was taking a week's leave to look after a seriously ill relation, and after some thought, added a few notes about which clients could have appointments later, and who might best look after the clients she needed to see but couldn't meet with.

Staying in the armchair instead of lying on the bed and risking falling asleep, she Googled "Paul Strong", which felt slightly odd seeing he was only a couple of metres away in her bed and with no idea what she was doing, but it had to be done. Knowing who his family were, in case she needed to contact someone, was her original motivation, but she found enough random information to keep her busy for half an hour. A newspaper article about a coroner's court hearing when his wife committed suicide a couple of years earlier shocked her, and inevitably made her wonder if his wife killed herself over his infidelities, if those rumours were true. She shook herself and felt she was being as nosy and despicable as that woman she had heard gossiping in the café and continued reading the next article about his graduation from law school, in a year when just under ten percent were so called mature students who had come from established careers. Paul was mentioned as "Paul Strong, formerly a paramedic". How ironic, she thought, seeing how useful he's already been to me and here I am, totally unskilled and bumbling my way through trying to take care of him.

After another session of wiping him with cold water and struggling to make him drink, she lay down again, put one hand on his arm and went to sleep despite her intention not to. At an early hour of the morning, she woke up when she felt his arm pull away from under her hand and sat up. 'What's wrong, what are you doing?'

'Toilet,' he said and tried to lever himself up, but she was off the bed in a flash and around to his side, holding him down with a hand on each of his shoulders. 'Not on you own! Stay sitting until we work out how to do this. Remember I can't get you off the floor if you keel over. Let me be your walking stick.'

Carefully helping him to his feet made her wonder how long she could look after him before they had an accident. His weight and height made supporting him a risky business and if he stumbled she might not be able to hold him up. Slowly they made it to the bathroom where she positioned him backed up against the edge of the toilet and said, 'No nonsense now, please! Hold onto the wall, for a moment.' She pulled his boxer shorts down and said, 'Sit down. And shout when you're finished. I'll come and be your walking stick again.'

The expression on his face made her laugh, despite how tired and worried she was. Outrage doesn't even begin to describe it, she thought, and if he wasn't so ill, he'd be pushing me away and refusing, but he's too weak to fight me off. Will he ever forgive me for all the humiliation I've caused him?

Standing outside the open bathroom door she heard him mumbling stray phrases to himself and realised he was confused again and might even have forgotten where he was, and possibly that she was there with him. Hoping these episodes of confusion were due to exhaustion and not anything more serious, she listened until she was sure he was finished and then went in to help him to his feet.

Once he was back in the bed, she tried to sound confident and calm, but her concern about how he alternated between seeming clarity and confusion made it hard to sound normal. She tried her best to make her voice cheerful and confident and said, 'Now drink some more, please, and then go back to sleep. I'll be right beside you.'

Momentarily his eyes were clear, though his voice was hoarse, and he was short of breath after the exertion. 'Thank you!'

'While you're here, I have power over you,' she said and smiled down at him, trying to inject some light-hearted nonsense into this dire situation.

'You always did.' His eyes closed and he seemed to fall immediately to sleep, leaving her staring down at his flushed face. Remembering how chapped and dry his lips had looked in the bright light of the bathroom, she got the lip balm out from the drawer in the bedside table. She sat down on the edge of the bed and rubbed some on his lips, very gently so as not to wake him. 'Your lips are like fish scales,' she whispered and ran her forefinger over his lips again and again, feeling her fingertip softening the waxy substance further, making it work better. 'I bet it's painful – you poor thing.' When he stirred and mumbled disconnected words, she leaned down, put her cheek against his and whispered, 'It's **OK**, I'm here with you, I've got you, you're safe, just go to sleep.'

That afternoon she managed to get hold of the senior partner in his firm after more online research. 'He's got a bad dose of the 'flu,' she said, only identifying herself as a family friend. 'He's running a very high temperature, and I think it's unlikely he'll be back at work for a week.'

By the time dusk once again dimmed the light from the window, Sofia had repeated the cycle of tasks so many times that she couldn't keep track. The only thing she was sure of was that she must be getting enough fluids into him, because the excruciating trip to the bathroom had taken place twice more. She lay down on the bed with her merino rug over her, put a hand on Paul's arm and fell into an exhausted sleep that lasted four hours. She woke in dark room with no lights on apart from the bud-lights draped on the windowsill behind the armchair and lay still, initially disorientated about which side of the bed she was on and trying to remember what she was meant to do. But apart from giving him water nothing occurred to her, so she scraped together enough energy to turn the bedside light on and get up, walked around the bed and gave Paul some water, wiped his face and collapsed on the bed again.

Chapter 25

By late Monday afternoon, she was in a brain fog of exhaustion and lack of food and forced herself to eat something, knowing that if she collapsed there would be nobody to look after Paul. She had taken his temperature while he slept an hour earlier and been relieved to see it was down to just over thirty-eight, and feeling slightly optimistic, she had eaten a piece of toast and drunk a cup of coffee standing by the kitchen bench.

When she returned to the bedroom, the sight of him threw her into a state of shock. He was lying on his back, perfectly still, his face was pale, and she knew he was dead. Instantly devastated she fell to her knees beside the bed and buried her face in the sheet beside his chest, sobbing, 'No, no, no – please don't do this to me, please – I need you.'

Then a hand touched the arm she had flung across his chest and Paul said weakly, 'What's happened? Are you crying?' and then she really cried. She put her head down again and cried, from a mixture of relief and tiredness and gratitude that he hadn't died. When she finally stopped, she lifted her head and said in a tear-thickened voice, 'I thought you were dead!'

'Silly girl - come and lie down,' he said, his voice depleted as if he was only half the man he normally was.

They slept until midnight when Sofia woke to find Paul trying to pull the covers over himself. She got up and sorted the bedding out, felt his forehead and smiled to herself in the dark. His skin was cool, he was not perspiring, and his breathing was no longer as uneven as it had been earlier. Getting back under the duvet in her clothes, she put her head on the pillow and barely noticed his arm coming over her body and pulling her closer.

Sofia woke with a jump, when something clattered in the kitchen and saw that Paul was not in the bed beside her. Standing yawning in the doorway she watched him fill his glass with water, once again back in his sweat-smelling T-shirt, his silhouette outlined by the dawn light.

'How are you feeling? Please come back to bed, you really shouldn't be up.'

He turned and said, 'I feel so weak – I don't know what happened last night. Some kind of terrible bug took hold of me. I'm sorry I caused all this trouble.'

She walked across and took his hand. 'Come on, we'll talk in bed. I don't want you to stand here and get chilled, and I want to take your temperature.'

He looked puzzled but followed her and let her push him down on the bed and pull the covers up.

'But then I must go home,' he said. 'I've got to get organised for a meeting I have first thing on Monday morning that I haven't finished preparing for.'

She sat down on the edge of the bed and said gently, 'It's actually Tuesday morning, not Saturday.'

The look on his face was priceless and over the next few minutes her explanations and his reactions made her laugh. Persuading him that he had somehow compressed three days into one was too much for him to believe at first, but she held up her make-up mirror and he had to accept that stubble like that didn't grow overnight.

'Now, listen,' she said, 'there's no need for you to worry about anything, I've organised a week's sick leave for you, I talked to your boss on Sunday, or it might have been Saturday, and I've taken sick leave too, so I can look after you. And now we'll get you cleaned up, well, we both need cleaning up, we're quite smelly - and I'll lend you a dressing gown and then we'll have breakfast.'

She walked to the bathroom beside him, put a clean towel on the basin and stood watching him through the open bathroom door as he got into the shower, and a moment later she was very glad she had. Paul turned the shower on and then made a grab for the wall with one hand, and she could see how weak he was, just about to slide to the floor, so she quickly pulled her clothes off and stepped into the walk-in shower.

'Lean against the wall and I'll give you a hand,' she said and tried not to laugh at his expression. 'I need a shower too and I want to wash my hair, but I'll do you first.'

The poor guy, she thought, he's been stripped not only of his clothes while practically unconscious, now he's being stripped of his privacy and manhandled like a baby. And he probably wonders what else has been going on that he can't remember.

Without listening to his protests and ignoring his free hand trying to ward her off, she rubbed soap into her hands and washed him from top to toe. At the end of a couple of minutes he was leaning heavily against the tiled wall on the brink of collapse again, so she decided that having been hosed down while she manoeuvred around him was enough of a shower for herself, rinsed them both off and said, 'Just hang on now – don't fall over just yet.'

Dripping wet she dragged the chair over from the corner by the handbasin and said, 'Sit down, please, there's a chair right behind you.' The fact that there were no objections from him while she dried him, standing wet and naked in front of him without even thinking of it, was proof of how tired he was. Not until he was sitting in the armchair in her bedroom, dressed in her much too small dressing gown, did she dry herself properly, squeeze the water out her hair and get into clean clothes. Only later would it occur to her that getting into the shower with him and casually getting dressed in front of him without a thought, was a measure of how their shared experience had brought them close, bypassing some normal steps on the way.

'Sorry,' she said and threw the towel on the floor, 'but you can't get back in bed just yet – stay where you are, this will only take a couple of minutes.'

She stripped the bed, made it again with clean

sheets, and went to put his clothes and the sheets in the washing machine.

'You are without a doubt the most efficient person I've ever met,' he said when she returned to the bedroom, and she was pleased to see he had got back into the bed under his own steam and looked slightly better. 'I can't imagine what you've had to do for me for the last however many days it is. You must be exhausted. I only remember bits and pieces.'

She looked searchingly at him and wondered what exactly he remembered, but all she said was, 'We'll have a sleep after breakfast. I've muted my phone, and I found yours and turned it right off. I didn't want it to disturb us earlier, but you probably want to check it now – I'll get it for you, I charged it with my cord. And put some of this on your lips – I used it on you earlier, you need it.'

She put the stick of lip balm into his hand and went to make breakfast.

Side by side in the bed with a tray between them they ate toast with plum jam and drank coffee, checking who had called and responding to messages on their phones. A couple of times Sofia glanced at Paul and thought how odd this felt, like a married couple with a routine; the second time he looked over and saw her smile. 'Yes? Is it the stubble?'

'God, no – I'll lend you a razor when you're fit

enough to stand unsupported for more than two minutes. I was just thinking how lucky it is that I've got several lovely frozen meals, so we can have for dinner tonight without me having to go out.'

'And what was the smile about?' He was teasing, she could see the corner of his mouth tweak up, though he tried to hide it.

'Nothing,' she said casually. 'I just felt like smiling because you're getting better.'

'Liar,' he said and moved the tray further over her way before he slid down in the bed. 'You're not very good at being evasive, are you?'

She didn't reply, just put the tray on the floor on her side, lay down and was asleep within seconds.

Chapter 26

It was evening after another beautiful day neither of them had seen. The sun had moved in its prescribed arc across the sky, spring had taken another step forward, and they had slept right through it.

Sitting at the kitchen counter, now half-dressed in his clean T-shirt and with a towel wrapped around his middle, Paul watched Sofia making dinner, which consisted of opening packets of frozen meals, putting them in the microwave oven and placing plates and various things in front of him.

'I don't cook,' she said and shot him a sideways glace. 'Never when I'm on my own, which is of course nearly all the time. I've been known to do something from a recipe if I've invited someone in, but I normally I try to avoid it.'

He laughed. 'I don't mind – I'm just grateful you're feeding me. I think I need thousands of calories to make up for the weight I've lost in the last few days.'

She glanced across at him, comparing him to what he had looked like that first day in the café, when she had studied his face and wondered if she had been wrong about him being sarcastic.

'You do look thinner,' she said. 'Some liquid calories might be good, so let's have a glass of wine with our dinner.' She walked around him to get glasses from the shelf beside him, and as she turned to put them on the breakfast counter tears pooled suddenly in her eyes, apparently for no reason, and she came to a halt with the glasses still in her hand. Paul looked up. 'What's wrong?'

'I don't know, it's nothing - don't worry, it's just some late reaction, I think.' She hesitated, unable to explain why this sudden emotion had overcome her now that things were nearly back to normal. She had held herself together through all the worry and lack of sleep, and it seemed like admitting a weakness to give way to tears now that it was over, and he was safe. She put the glasses down, and he reached for her hand and pulled her towards him. 'Come here,' he said fand put his arm around her. 'Tell me what's wrong.'

Sofia leaned her head against his and sighed. 'I truly don't know. I think the whole thing's just catching up with me. I was so worried, no, I was terrified, and I kept thinking maybe I was doing the wrong thing and I should just call for an ambulance, but it seemed to be at least under control, and I didn't want them to …' Her voice tapered off and she knew she should have stopped before those last few words because now he would want to know what she had nearly said. She lifted her head and moved a step away, embarrassed and unwilling to reveal her feelings.

'You didn't want them to - what?'

'It was just that I knew if I called them, they'd take you away and I wouldn't be there to talk to you and make you feel safe – you were so muddled at times, you went from being very clear and nearly normal to being confused, so you didn't know where you were or who was doing things to you.'

She stopped for a moment, embarrassed by what she was confessing, knew she knew she had said too much and tried to make light of it. 'But I could always calm you, settle you down and stop you being so anxious.' She tried to laugh. 'Such self-delusion! As if I'm irreplaceable.'

'You are,' he said, and fixed her with a look and made it impossible for her to move away. 'To me, you *are* irreplaceable. Would you please move closer, so I don't have to stand up and lose my towel and feel ridiculous?'

She stood beside the stool with her head once again leaning against his and his arm around her and wondered if what he had just said was as significant as it had sounded, and what it might mean in the context of his other woman, and then the drier let out it's five penetrating high-pitched beeps and they both jumped.

'That's the sheets and your boxers and socks!' she said and started to laugh. 'I'll get your stuff out right away, so you can put them on warm from the drier. I'd left them in the washing machine when I got your T-shirt out, which I wanted dry as soon as possible. I knew nothing of mine would fit you.'

After vegetarian lasagne and vanilla ice cream with Bayley's poured over it, Sofia said, 'Let's sit in the sitting room, maybe read some online news or something. We seem to be out of step with normal life today, sleeping in the day and getting up in the evening. Would you like another glass of wine? OK – I'll just go to the bathroom first.'

She made a detour to the bedroom and got the thermometer from the bedside table before she returned to the living room with their wine glasses.

'Open your mouth!' she said and poked the

thermometer in before he could protest and remained beside him ready to grab it as soon as it beeped. Now that he was rapidly getting better, she didn't want to give him a chance to conceal anything from her by not letting her see it.

'Thirty-seven point two! That's good – I think you're on the mend.'

'Patsy Sylvester is your mother, isn't she?' he said after a while, looking up from reading something on his phone. 'I love her voice – I've saw her in The Barber of Seville a couple of years ago.'

'Yes, she is – how did you know? I mean, we've got different surnames.'

'I was curious about where the Garnier came from, so I Googled you, read about your French father who drowned when you were a little girl and discovered that Patsy Sylvester is your mother. Did you Google me?'

That secret amusement was there again and now she knew how to detect it, which might be very useful in the future, if they had a future, which was probably unlikely.

'I did, while you were really sick, just in case.' She remembered how she had worried about what she would do, who to contact, how to explain to ambulance people that she knew very little about him and nothing whatever about his next of kin.

'And what did you find?' Now he sounded serious, and she was caught hesitating about how much to tell him.

'Did you read about my wife?'

Thank God, he said it, so I didn't have to, she thought, it would have been such a difficult thing to bring up. 'Yes, I did. A newspaper article, just a short paragraph.'

'She gave birth and the baby died in the delivery room,' he said slowly, as if he was considering how much to tell her. 'And then she became depressed and took long leave and went to stay with her father in Christchurch, and he didn't realise how bad she was, though I had warned him and told him what her doctor had said – and then it was too late. She took an overdose of some medication they had prescribed for her and drowned in the bath one night. She left a note for her dad.'

That last piece of information took her by surprise and his expression told her nothing. He had effectively said that his wife had not left a note for him, but why had he told her? To make her ask, or was there more to come? Suddenly she felt terrified that she might say the wrong thing and chose a safe option.

'I'm so sorry – dreadful for you, a double loss. It must have been hard.'

'The baby wasn't mine.' His face revealed nothing of what he felt, it was a bald statement of fact, and it left Sofia in the same quandary as before; none of the multitude of options that flashed through her mind seemed appropriate.

'I knew ahead of time,' he continued. 'She told me as soon as she found out she was pregnant that she was having an affair with a colleague at work, and she didn't know if I or the other guy was the father, so it got complicated. She didn't want a divorce, and he didn't want to live with her. For him it was just a workplace fling, so I said we'd bring the baby up as if it was ours and not do a DNA check if that's what she wanted.'

They were silent for a long time, neither of them looking at the other, and Sofia thought how strange it was that the silence this time didn't feel awkward, not as if they were avoiding a tricky subject. It felt more as if two people, who understood each other, were contemplating something from the past and there was no need to say anything.

Finally, he took a sip of wine and looked across the coffee table at her, his gaze direct and serious. 'I no longer loved her when she died – she had killed the feeling I had for her. She was openly mercenary about her reasons for not wanting a divorce and not wanting to bring up a child on her own. She said "if you love me it will work" – but it didn't. I never said that it wasn't going to work because I didn't love her or anything like it, though. When she got so depressed, her dad said he wanted her to come and stay, so she wasn't alone in the house all day – he's retired – and she went to Christchurch, and we never got to discuss it again.'

He paused and then he said rapidly, as if he worried he would change his mind if he didn't get the words out quickly, 'I've never understood why I agreed to continue with the marriage, to bring the baby up together whether it was mine or not. When I think of it now, it's like I somehow imagined things would go back to what they had been. As if we could just forget it and carry on, like married friends. But looking back I realise I could never have done that - it was over. Thank God, I didn't tell her, or I might have felt I was the reason she killed herself.'

'How did you know the baby wasn't yours?' Sofia hoped this question wouldn't overstep whatever boundary still existed between them, but she found it interesting and wondered if he had asked for a post-mortem DNA. Somehow the possibility that he had done that frightened her, as if it would change her perception of his character and possibly destroy their relationship.

'It was perfectly clear that the baby had an Asian

parent, either Chinese or Japanese – I saw it and so did the nurses. One of them took me aside soon after he was born, thinking I was taken by surprise, that I hadn't expected it and was upset. She could probably see all kinds of problems coming up for us, but though my wife hadn't told me, I had wondered if her lover was her Japanese colleague, whose wife was still in Japan. She used to talk about him a lot and quote funny things he said, so to some degree I was alerted before she got pregnant and had to tell me. And I've wondered if she would have told me at all, if her lover hadn't been Japanese, if there was no chance that the baby's appearance would be impossible to hide. Would she have just quietly pretended the baby was definitely ours? I can't even guess.'

Reluctant to ask anything more and uncertain about changing the subject, Sofia made no comment, just watched him as he sat staring down into the wineglass in his hand.

'Do you know what the hardest thing was?' he said after a while. 'It was pretending I was grieving for my son and responding to people's sympathy. I felt like a sham. Not that it wasn't a sad event – it would have been whoever the parents were - but having to face the assumption from everyone that it was my child was very difficult.'

He's amazing, she thought and looked across at that handsome face that so rarely revealed his feelings. How many men could have endured that situation without telling the truth? He didn't love her, but he supported the lie because she was depressed, and they were in a very difficult situation. And possibly nobody knows even now, apart from Paul and me – his capacity for integrity and compassion is off the scale.

And then she wondered if he had told his lover all this, or if he was keeping his new relationship separate from the tragedy, and if she herself was really the only person he had told. I'm at risk now, she thought, because I feel so close to him and I can't get tangled up with him - it wouldn't be good for me, so I must conceal what I feel and never let him see I feel differently about him than he does about me.

Chapter 27

The mood was broken by Sofia's phone buzzing, and she took the call without looking to see who it was, distracted by his story and not realising that the phone was on speaker. Why is it still on speaker, she thought, what has Bitsy done that I can't seem to undo? Some contacts on speaker, like Marcus the other day and others not.

'Sofia, *why* do you never tell me anything? I can't believe I had to find out from your secretary that you're on sick leave for a whole week! How are you?' Patsy's voice was three quarters affronted and one quarter concerned.

Now Sofia was stuck between her instinctive wish to turn the speaker function off, and how it might look to Paul if she did, as if she didn't trust him to listen to a conversation between herself and her mother.

'Oh, nothing very dramatic, just a really bad cough and a bit of a temperature, but I'm getting better already, so I'll probably go back to work tomorrow. You know how it is with me and coughs, sometimes they take over my life.'

'OK, that's good! I hear the birthday dinner for Fliss was a success, she sent an email thanking me for the present. Did she manage to dress like a civilised human being, or did she turn up at Logan Brown looking like some crazy hippie geriatric?'

'Oh, for goodness' sake, mum – of course she dressed nicely. She had a gorgeous dark red velvet dress a friend of hers had made for her. She looked very glamorous. And so did Summer, who now has bright green hair.'

She was not about the tell Patsy that the velvet dress was in fact a kaftan that trailed on the floor behind Fliss, and that it had something that resembled gold cowboy fringes along the outside of the sleeves, a garment that attracted a lot of attention.

'Now,' said her mother on a note of determination. 'I've been thinking about that letter granddad gave you, and how you said we can't open it until he's dead and that you've put it in your vault or whatever it's called. Of course, we can open it! He's got dementia, his word doesn't count, does it? So be a good girl and open it as soon as you're back at work and then call me and tell me what all the fuss was about.'

A few minutes later and having only just managed to restrain herself from shouting at her mother, Sofia ended the call.

'I'm sure you love her singing voice,' she said, exasperated and feeling exhausted after repeating everything several times. 'Everybody does. But as you heard, her speaking voice and what she says can drive you to the verge of despair. Reason doesn't register when she hell-bent on having her own way, and she had already driven me crazy about this. She's the centre of her own universe and assumes she is also the centre of not just mine but everyone else's as well. And if I gave way, I would be reduced to slave status, probably forever. She's a manipulator of the highest order.'

Paul laughed, but he was clearly curious. 'Is it one of those letters with "only to be opened after my death" on it? I've never come across one of those.'

She drank some of her wine and used the little pause to decide what to tell him, put the glass down slowly and had still not decided. She did trust him totally and knew he might have good advice to give, but was she ready to reveal the whole truth to anyone at all? Paul had been watching her and she suddenly realised that he had picked up on her hesitation. And now he'll wonder if I don't trust him, she thought, which would be awful after what he told me in confidence just before.

'I think I'd better show you rather than just try to tell you,' she said and got up. 'I folded the envelope when I put it in my bag at the resthome, it was quite big, and then it fell apart when I pulled it out, when I got home from Masterton – that's where he is. The glue on the flap had given up and it all just tumbled out on the floor. And I read it, because the first thing I saw was a mysterious newspaper cutting from 1962 and I couldn't resist reading it.'

Picking up her laptop from the table in the bedroom, she brought it through to the living room, printed the file she had saved and stood holding the pages before she handed them to him. 'I think he put all the stuff in that envelope long ago and only wrote "Important" on it, and then much later he added "For Sofia". There was nothing written down about keeping it until after his death, that's just what he told me, several times. And I didn't put everything back in the envelope after reading it - I held on to a couple of pages. But I scanned the lot and saved it in this PDF file I've just printed out for you. The newspaper cutting and the two A4 pages are still here in my desk drawer, the rest is in the envelope in our safe at work, the harmless stuff. We can discuss that later, but I want you to read it all first.'

She sat back sipping her wine and watched him reading, wondering what was going through his mind, and what he would say about her having kept the two main pages, but when he finished the last page, he didn't even look up, he started again from the beginning. She went to her desk and got the manila folder with the handwritten pages and put them on the coffee table in front of him and again sat down to watch him.

I could watch him forever, she thought, it sounds so silly, but it's true. There's something about the way he concentrates, like when he bandaged my finger, as if he radiates competence and calm, and right now I can feel my hand wanting to reach out to touch him.

'It's an extraordinary story, a love story' said Paul slowly and put the papers on the table. 'Did they remain happily together from then on?'

'Oh yes, grandma died three years ago, and I think they loved each other right through their life together. Sometimes when we were together for family events, they looked at each other when others were talking, as if they were alone or not listening. I noticed it even as a child, they had something special that bound them together. As I grew up, I sometimes felt that they didn't really need anyone else, we as family were of interest and they loved us, but they only really *needed* each other.'

She paused and wondered why she had never mentioned this feeling to anyone before, never said it to anyone in the family and now she was telling Paul. She gave herself a little mental shake and continued. 'And those notes – the first time I read them they brought tears to my eyes. The tenderness and the fact that they wrote those notes to each other at all – I mean, how many people would do that? I'm sure the first couple from him were because he was concerned about her, thinking of her being alone at home all day, depressed and with two tiny children while he was at work – plus the impact on her of having killed a man. And instead of saying it, or perhaps instead of only saying it, he wrote those notes and if she felt battered by what had happened, she could pick the note up and read it again when he wasn't there and know he was thinking of her.'

She reached for the printed pages and looked at the images of those notes and thought of the young man who had stood in the kitchen early in the mornings writing them, and what his thoughts must have been.

'About his wish to keep these private until after

his death,' said Paul slowly. 'I wonder if it's still that he's protecting her – not that he's protecting himself. But even so, he wants the family at least to know the truth eventually.'

'And I've been wondering if perhaps they *never* talked about it, but they shared their feelings via those notes that reveal nothing of the background, of what started it all. So that's all I left in the envelope, the notes - nothing incriminating, nothing that would give my mother cause to think her career and reputation are about to be ruined. And nothing that my aunt Fliss, the hippie from Golden Bay, might feel was interesting enough to share on social media or on her website. She might think a bit of drama would be good PR. I kind of felt I wanted to protect them both, I mean my grandparents – not turn their tragedy and love into something else.'

'And what does Fliss do? What's her website about?'

Sofia laughed. 'You'll never guess, so I'll tell you - she paints portraits of people's pets from photos. She's very good, and she earns a lot of money. Sometimes she paints them on black velvet mounted in fancy gold frames – particularly deceased cats - and people pay a fortune for them. But to go back to the papers in grandad's envelope - what do you think

I should do? I could put the cutting and those pages he wrote, the story itself, back in the envelope.'

'Knowing you, I'm sure you did some research – about the drifter, I mean. Did you find anything?'

'Nope, nothing that identifies him. I did get the address of where they lived from Fliss just recently when she was here for her birthday, the name of the street and the number, which I couldn't remember – they lived in Trentham. I used the pretext that I thought I might go there and take a photo of the house to give to grandad. I said he'd talked about how he hadn't seen the place for twenty years.'

'And did you?'

'No, I *was* going to go and check it out this last weekend, but I didn't have time,' she said coolly. 'A friend of mine was very ill, and I've been looking after him since Friday.'

'You're such a good girl!' said Paul and grinned. 'Let's find it on Google Earth - this is like an adventure. And can I have another glass of wine please?'

The sat side by side at the little dining table with Sofia's laptop and she typed the address into the search engine, hit enter and they watched in silence as the satellite image zoomed in on Trentham. 'There it is, look, the garage is still there at the side,' said Sofia. 'If it's the original one we must decide that we should do.'

'Of course,' he said as if he assumed they were in this together, and it made her smile. She changed from the aerial view to the street view and rotated the angle so they could look straight at the front of the house. 'Yep, that's definitely the original garage – look at those wooden doors that open in two halves with a padlock on a bracket. Nobody's built a garage door like that for decades. And the house looks as if nothing much has changed either.'

Then she looked at him and realised he looked tired again and said, 'I think you should lie down - you're looking very tired again. This isn't something you recover from right away, I wouldn't think. Why don't you lie down on the bed, and I'll sit in the armchair in there and we can continue talking about it.'

She was surprised that he agreed and thought he must be really tired not to protest at all. She turned the bedside lights on and the string of bud-lights at the window.

'They *are* real!' exclaimed Paul from the bed, where he sat leaning against the headboard with his half-drunk glass of wine in his hand. 'I remember it, I thought it was a dream - someone wrapped in a rug with tiny lights around them, watching over me – it was such a nice sight, like a painting. I thought I dreamt it.'

She smiled without saying anything, blinked back the tears that threatened to overflow and took a sip from her nearly empty wineglass.

'I think you can overlook the ethics of concealing those two pages and the cutting,' said Paul after a few minutes, while Sofia had sat silently watching his eyelids droop and then lift again, wondering if she should take the glass out of his hand before he fell asleep sitting up. 'It's not as if it would make any difference to anyone, no inheritance lost, no assets to claim. Maybe seal those pages in a separate envelope and carry on the tradition, leave it in safe keeping with instructions that it's only to be opened after your own death?'

'That's a good idea,' she said after considering for a moment. 'And it will make me feel more comfortable about not leaving them in the original envelope - I can feel I haven't permanently hidden evidence.'

'I wouldn't tell anyone, though,' said Paul. 'And I mean not anyone at all. People love a tasty bit of gossip, and you know what they say, everyone thinks telling just one other person in strict confidence is OK, and then that person tells another and so it goes on. Like that story about the hen who lost a feather, and it became a news story about a hen who lost all her feathers and died from cold.'

'Really? I never heard of a story about a hen losing a feather. Where did you get this from? Or did you make it up?'

'Hans Christian Andersen,' said Paul, with a look on his face as if he found it hard to believe she didn't know this. 'But to get back to the confession letters – I have no moral problem with sealing them up separately, and you know you can trust me not to talk.'

'It might become a family tradition.' She smiled at the thought. 'One generation after another passing the envelope on. And you're right – there is nobody to prosecute, they didn't know who that tramp was sixty years ago, and there's even less chance of finding out now. There really *is* nothing to be gained from reporting it.'

Relief flowed through her; he had accepted her reasoning that nothing would be achieved by making the story public and was prepared to keep the secret. In the back of her mind, she had worried that he, as a prosecutor, would insist that she stick to the ethics and the legal obligations, but he hadn't.

Chapter 28

When Sofia woke up the bed beside her was empty, but she could hear the shower, so she put her dressing gown on and went to the kitchen to make coffee. When Paul appeared, he was fully dressed apart from shoes, and Sofia suddenly felt awkward, as if he was a stranger instead of the man in boxershorts she had tended to for days.

'You look good today! I'm just making coffee,' she said. 'If you make some toast, I'll have a quick shower and get dressed.'

She was back in the kitchen in record time because the disparity between them that she had suddenly felt when he turned up dressed, made her feel she must re-establish some kind of equality, to quickly make herself feel less at a disadvantage. While she showered and dressed, she had tried to understand why she had felt that urgency. She knew she was getting overly aware of him and admitted to herself that she had fallen in love with him, but now everything seemed so odd. After such intimacy for days and nights, now what? Were they back to some kind of previous state, friends maybe, very close, but no more than friends? She told herself that the little signs of affection from Paul's side were probably no more than those he might display towards any woman he was very fond of and grateful to, and she reminded herself not to show what she felt. There was no way she was cut out to be one of many love interests, however much she wanted him.

They had breakfast in the living room with the balcony door open to the sunny morning, both reading news, discussing occasional items of interest they came across, but otherwise not talking much. The call from Patsy took Sofia by surprise, and she realised too late that she hadn't explored the settings on her phone to find out why Patsy's calls were always on speaker.

'Just checking you've recovered from your cold,' said Patsy breezily. 'You do sound better. And one other thing that I forgot to ask you yesterday - that man who fixed your finger, have you seen him since?'

'I had coffee with him so he could inspect the finger for himself,' said Sofia and avoided looking at

Paul. 'And the finger's right back to normal, which is wonderful because it means I can type fast again. I kept forgetting and spent a lot of time flinching and moaning – it's the disadvantage of having taught myself to touch-type.'

But her attempt to divert Patsy failed. 'What's his name?' she asked as soon as Sofia stopped talking. 'He looked *very* handsome in that photo on FaceBook. Are you going to see him again? Did he seem interested?'

'I have no idea – I suppose I might bump into him at some stage, and no, he didn't seem interested in me. I think it was just professional interest, mum – like, he put the finger back into its whatever you call those bits, socket or something. And then he felt he should check it hadn't gone wrong in some way.'

As soon as she ended the call, she rose to get more coffee and stood with her back to the sitting room while she waited for the jug to boil. Behind her Paul made no comment, and when she turned to ask if he wanted a top-up, she had calmed down.

'I'd like to go to have a look at that house in Trentham,' she said casually. 'I must take a photo of it now because I promised Fliss I would, and she's texted me the full address. Would you like to come?'

The way he studied her face before he replied could have meant anything, but after a moment he said, 'I'd like to go for a drive - anywhere at all really. Provided you do the driving because I don't think I quite trust myself and my reaction times just yet.'

They set out straight after breakfast and found the house in Trentham looking exactly as it had on Google Earth, a pale green, nineteen-fifties bungalow with the front door in the centre with a window each side, one bigger than the other, and a short concrete driveway ending in a single-car garage.

Parking the car on the other side of the street they got out and stood looking at it for a moment, then Paul said, 'It's like an illustration in a picture book, very nineteen-fifties. I don't think anyone's opened those garage doors for a while. The padlock looks rusted even from here.'

They crossed the street and Sofia got her phone out and was about to take a photo when an old man came limping around the corner of the house next door. 'Are you looking for someone?' He stared hard at Sofia. 'Are you taking pictures?'

'Yes, I am,' she said and walked closer to the fence between them, smiling to make him less suspicious. 'My grandparents lived here when they were first married and now my grandfather's in a resthome, and he wanted me to come and take a picture of the house for him. My name's Sofia Garnier.'

'How long ago would that have been?' asked the old man, interested now, and leaned on the fence as if he was settling in for a long chat. 'What's his name? I might have known him.'

'His name is Sylvester,' said Sofia, deliberately not saying if this was his first name or his surname. 'I know they lived here in nineteen-sixty-one when my mother was born, but I don't know when they moved from here to Masterton – probably just a few years later.'

'I wouldn't know him then,' said the old man. 'We bought this place in the late seventies. Mrs Stockwell isn't home, she works at the primary school – she's some kind of volunteer helper, but if you want to have a look around, I'm sure it would be fine with her. I'll tell her you came and who you are.'

At the spur of the moment Sofia said, 'Grandad is forgetting a lot of things now, and I thought it would be nice for him to have a photo to look at, you know, to maybe remember a few more things. I know they were happy here and both their children were born in that house.'

'Maybe take a photo at the back as well, I mean the back of the house,' said the man. 'If the poor old chap is getting forgetful it might bring some memories back, as you say. You're a good girl to think of him.'

The back garden was as tidy as the front with a round bed of roses in the centre of the lawn and an orange tree in the corner behind the garage. Sofia took two more photos, one of the house itself and one of the garage.

'Look at the corner,' said Paul quietly as they stood there on Mrs Stockwell's perfectly manicured lawn with the neighbour no longer watching them. 'The left-hand rear corner, that's where he dug the deeper hole. And not a crack in the concrete, no sign of anything strange. Isn't it amazing, we're the only ones who know there is a body buried there.'

'Don't forget the frying pan! And granddad knows – somewhere in the back of his brain is the memory of it. I don't think I'll show him the photos – what if he suddenly starts talking about it and someone reports it?'

As they drove away Paul said, 'You've got a way with you, as my mum would say. The way you get people to relate to you – it's a gift. That man went from being ready to call the cops to being your friend in thirty seconds. I didn't dare open my mouth in case I ruined it.'

'But on the other hand, if he'd suddenly had a heart attack you would have known how to save his life, and that's a gift too.'

Back at the turn-off to the highway, she said

impulsively, 'Shall we drive over the Remutaka Hill? Have coffee at Greytown?'

'Yes please, I've never driven north this way.' Paul chuckled. 'And seeing we're both on sick leave and can do what we want so long as nobody spots us, why not. If we see someone we know, we'll say we're on proper leave.'

'Who the hell came up with the idea to call this a hill? It's a proper mountain,' he said when they started up the steep road over the Remutaka hill, where the tight bends revealed a new perspective at every turn and the winding road skirting the edges of deep gorges and ravines clad in native bush. 'What a spectacular road!'

'My cousin Storm says it's his favourite driving road – he's one of those men who talk endlessly about cars and only buy very fast ones. And when he mentions his car, he doesn't just say what make it is – like "when I was parking the Volvo" – he mentions the model *and* whatever litter of letters comes after that. You know how models of some cars come with alphabet soup after the name.'

Paul chuckled again, and she smiled at the sound of him so cheerful and obviously back to nearly normal. 'What does Storm do? Something to do with cars?'

'He's a stockbroker in Sydney and rapidly adding

to this middle-age spread. Storm and his younger sister are much older than I am, because Fliss had her babies very young and my mum didn't. I love Storm, his like an older brother in a way, and we've always been very close. He's a very kind man and often very funny, but he would be an absolute menace to live with. His wife said once, just before she left him, that being married to Storm was like permanently residing in a bar combined with a car dealer's display room, where the entry requirement was a large dollop of brinkmanship. And he can't whisper.'

'He can't whisper – or he won't?'

'No, he really can't, he never could. When we were kids, when I came back to live in New Zealand with mum after my father died, he was sixteen or seventeen and I was six and I used to spend ages when we met up trying to teach him to whisper – and failed.'

'I've never heard of anyone who couldn't whisper, it's extraordinary. Is his voice loud?'

'Very! He shares his opinions and stories with the entire restaurant when you go out for dinner with him – and his laugh is deafening at close range.'

Chapter 29

After an early lunch in Greytown, Sofia took
Paul on a leisurely walk right down one side
of the picturesque main street and back up on the
other side.

'I know the wind is surprisingly cold,' she said,'
but the exercise will be good for you after being
cooped up for days on end, get your blood moving a
bit faster – and you have a jacket on. And I want you
to experience this little gem of a town seeing you've
never been here before. Not just the few surprisingly
grandiose building dotted around, that you wouldn't
expect to find here, but this whole lovely main street.'

His quiet chuckle made her feel special, as if only
she could make him do that, which was a delusion of
frightening proportions, she told herself, having once

again nearly been temped into wondering if they might have a future.

'As you must have gathered by now, I love this little town,' she said and stopped outside an antique store window. 'It's like it was specially designed to part you from as much of your money as possible. I mean, look at it! If it isn't delicatessen goods or artworks or wine, it's cafes and antique shops. The only way to handle it without spending too much, is to drive right through and have lunch at some boring café in another town.'

She moved a couple of steps to the left and said suddenly, 'Do you mind waiting for a moment – I can see something in there I want to have a look at.'

'I'll come in with you – this wind is getting colder by the minute.'

'In that case, would you mind creating a bit of a distraction? So I can sneakily check something without arousing interest?'

'Of course – let's split up as soon as we're inside the door. Whichever side you go to, I'll go the other way.'

Ten minutes later they were once again standing on the pavement looking in the window.

'Was it not what you thought,' asked Paul, 'or was it too expensive?'

'Both — I thought it might have been a Lalique bowl, but it's by Etling — he was an apprentice of Lalique's and made very similar things, also beautiful and valuable. I think they probably checked - it looks so much like Lalique that they would have turned it over to check, but they didn't research who Etling was. If they had, it would be a thousand or more instead of two hundred and fifty, because it's signed *and* numbered. But at the moment I'm not spending even that because I'm saving for a new car. I don't like borrowing money.'

He continued to look in through the shop window and said, 'Can you show me from here where it is? I'd like to have a look at it.'

'Move a bit further over — see that tall dresser, behind the low glass cabinet over at left the side? The bowl is on the right-hand side beside the tall vase, it's a low-profile bowl, nearly white, or maybe very pale bluish white.'

'Right, I can see it, probably a bit better than you can because I'm taller. It seems to have sculpted shapes underneath or are they feet?'

'It does — quite exaggerated rose or peony shapes, like they're half emerging out of the surface underneath. And when you look at it from the top you see them in various shades of white and nearly opalescent blue, depending on how thick the glass is in each part – very beautiful.'

He looked down at her and smiled. 'I can tell you love it - and if it had been Lalique, and if you hadn't been saving for a new car, would you have bought it? For however much *that* would have been, several thousand?'

'No, I certainly wouldn't! But I was very tempted when I saw it was signed by Etling and at that price. I literally had to grab hold of my hand to stop it picking the damn thing up and taking it to the counter.'

By the time they were back in Wellington, Paul was asleep in the passenger seat, which he had tilted right back as soon as they were over the Remutaka hill, and Sofia drove back to her flat and into the residents' underground parking without waking him.

He was still asleep when she turned the ignition off, and she sat for a long time looking at him, taking in his black and devilish eyebrows, his equally black eyelashes, and the way his hairline came to a peak at the centre of his forehead. I do love him, she thought, I really do, and it has nothing to do with how good looking he is. It's that calm and competent quality, the way he thinks before he answers, making that little pause as he studies your face as if to make sure he truly understands what you mean. But he's not for me, he's had so many opportunities to show it and he hasn't, so it's not love from his side. And that other relationship of his, how could I compete? It's not realistic to even think of it. I'll get him to stay for dinner, then I'll drop him off at his house, and that will be that. Just one more evening and then it's over.

Chapter 30

When Sofia turned the engine off, Paul sat up, suddenly wide awake. 'Hey! Where are we? Are we back in town already?'

'Back in the underground garage,' she said. 'I don't want to take you back to an empty house with nothing but sour milk in the fridge at this time of the day. We'll have a Japanese dinner and I'll drive you home afterwards. That gives you a few days to get on top of work and whatever – OK?'

Two minutes after Sofia unlocked the door, there were three quick knocks on the door. 'That will be Bitsy,' she said and returned to the hall. 'Hi, Bitsy, come in!'

In the living room Bitsy saw Paul standing by the balcony door and stopped, uncertain and suddenly shy. 'Who's that man?' she whispered.

'He's a friend,' whispered Sofia, bending down as if she was telling a secret. 'His name is Paul, and he is very kind. He's the one who fixed my finger – remember I told you about him and how clever he was.'

'Do I have to talk to him?'

'No, of course not. But he's very interested to hear you read – I've told him how you come from next door to practise your reading and how well you're reading now. And he knows stories, some of them are about hens and you said you like hens. Go and get the book out and I'll make some hot chocolate for us all.'

On the way to the kitchen, she made a detour past Paul, while Bitsy went to the study to get her book, and said quietly. 'Don't let on you have no idea who she is, please! I'll explain later.'

Bitsy and Sofia sat side by side at the table with their mugs of hot chocolate and the book, and Paul, who had looked quizzically at his mug when Sofia handed it to him, sat down opposite.

Ten minutes later, Sofia took Bitsy's hand and said, 'That was amazing, darling! You seem to have taken a giant leapt forward lately, instead of only one little step at a time. Any minute now you'll be better at reading than all the other kids in your class. Would you like to stay and have dinner with us? I can ask your mum if you like?'

Bitsy thought for a moment, a little crease between her eyebrows. 'What are you having?'

'Japanese food, from the restaurant down the street.'

'No, thanks, I'd rather have dinner at home – I don't like Japanese food,' said Bitsy politely and Sofia smiled. 'Have you ever had Japanese food?'

Bitsy shook her head. 'No, but it looks funny – I don't want to try – not today.' And then to Sofia's surprise, she looked across the table at Paul and said, 'Do you have any kids?'

He shook his head, but before he said anything Bitsy continued. 'Would you like to read to me instead of Sofia? It would be like a treat for you if you don't do that a lot, wouldn't it?'

She's fallen in love, thought Sofia as she watched Bitsy leading Paul to the sofa, and he he's hardly said a word, just smiled at her.

'So, this is how we sit when we read – you sit *there* in the middle, and I sit *here* in the corner, and then we put the flat blue cushion from the other corner on my legs so we can have the book flat, so we can both see the pictures – all right? Oh, no, we haven't got a book!' She giggled. 'We forgot to get a book!'

Paul, who seemed unperturbed by the role that

had been unexpectedly thrust upon him, said, 'I'll tell you a story instead of reading one. Do you think that would be OK? It's about a hen – no, it's about a whole lot of hens, let's say twenty-four.'

Sofia stood for a few minutes thinking and making a note on her shopping pad before she picked up the phone and ordered what she hoped was exactly what they had ordered the night Paul got sick. When she turned around the story was nearly at an end and Paul was saying, 'That's what happens if you repeat things you hear, if you don't get it right or if you add things.'

'Chinese whispers!' exclaimed Bitsy, delighted with herself. 'It's a bit like Chinese whispers – but my mum says it's a silly name and nobody does that in Singapore, and she doesn't know why it's called that. I must tell her about the hens that did it!'

When Bitsy had left Sofia turned to Paul. 'You handled that very well, I must say. She's very bossy – just lucky for you all she wanted was a story. Imagine building a fort of blankets and sitting on the floor with a torch waiting for imaginary daybreak so the wolves will stop howling outside – which was her reward last week.'

'I have a couple of nieces and nephews,' he said. 'I can handle a fort made of blankets, and imaginary wolves don't faze me at all. So, she lives next door?'

'Yes – her parents are immigrants, they came here before she was born. She's had trouble with her reading and her parents are always working or studying – or at the gym, so she comes here for reading training once a week.'

That night things felt different, and Sofia had not grasped quite how different until she had picked up their food order and was getting wine glasses out of the dishwasher. I'll only have one glass, she thought, because I'm driving him home after dinner, and then the contrast between the previous night and this one struck her with a force that made her feel devastated. The night before they had seemed like a couple, comfortable and relaxed, sharing confidences. Tonight, he was suddenly a guest, someone who would thank her, get out of her car and go inside his house, leaving her alone. She fought back the emotion and then jumped, when Paul said, as if he had read her mind, 'I'll take a taxi back. There's no need for you to get the car out again and drive me – and then you can have wine, too.'

From that moment until he left, she made a continuous effort to keep the sadness confined and invisible, unwilling to expose her feelings. When he was ready to go, she handed him his keys and wallet, which she had taken out of his jeans pockets when she folded his clothes that first night, and said, 'Don't forget these.' That simple act was nearly the tipping point, the seeming domesticity of it, the fact that she was reminding him, made her feel alone even before he had gone.

He stood behind her as she opened the door, and when she turned, he put both arms around her and held her tight against him. 'Thank you! You're an amazing girl – so kind and so patient. I'll never forget it. I'll be in touch!' He kissed her temple and let her go, and she closed the door behind him without responding, unable to speak. I feel as if I've lost him, she thought, but I never had him, I just borrowed him.

Chapter 31

The remedy for self-pity is keeping busy, so stop this damn agonising and do something practical, Sofia said out loud, and went back to the living room to start tidying up. By ten o'clock she had stripped the bed, put the sheets and towels through the washing machine and made the bed with fresh linen. She cleaned up in the kitchen, wiped every surface and turned the dishwasher on. She transferred the washing to the dryer before she dusted the entire flat, then stood in the middle of the living room wondering what she could do next.

The photo of the house in Trentham, of course! Initially, she had thought that she would print a copy for her grandfather and drive up to Masterton in the weekend and see if he recognised it. But now it felt safer not to give him any reminders about the time when he built the garage and what lay buried under the floor. There was no knowing what kind of random memories would come to the surface if he saw the photo, and she couldn't even guess what might develop from there. Would he start telling everybody around him about the dead man in the kitchen? Would he dredge up more and more detail until the story became too detailed to be brushed off as dementia ramblings, and then what? She couldn't bear to think that she would not only have betrayed his confidence, but that she was also the cause of trouble for him, the very thing he had tried to ensure would not happen until after his death.

She printed one copy of the photo to add to the archived material at work, and then wrote a long email to Fliss with copies to Storm and Summer, telling them about the visit to Trentham, what she had been doing since she saw them, and attached the photo. Thinking about work made her pause to reconsider if she really ought to put the confession pages into the envelope already in the archive, or even in an envelope to be opened after her own death. Just because she was only thirty-three did not mean the secret would be safe for a long time; she might be killed in a traffic accident a next month and her family would open the envelope, letting the genie out of the bottle. All the negative things that had initially made her hold those pages back were relevant whichever envelope the confession came out of.

After some thought, she wrote the address on the back of the photo and put it and the two confession pages into an envelope. The she searched the Internet for Paul's address and wrote on the outside of the envelope: 'To be given to my mother Patsy Sylvester after my death, and if she pre-deceases me, to be given to Paul Scott (prosecutor), who at this date lives at 74 High Street, Island Bay, Wellington.'

That should find him even decades from now, she thought, dated and signed it and then sat looking at it for a long time. Considering the short time she had known him, it seemed incredible that she could feel that she trusted him totally and knew he would do whatever was the right thing at the time. It was a strange feeling for someone like herself, who tended not to trust people, to doubt their motives and keep things to herself. He knows my earlier reservations, she thought, and he'll do something sensible if these things end up in his hands.

At half past one in the morning, Sofia went to bed and even after her determined attempts to keep busy in order to divert her sadness, she found it hard to go to sleep. Lying once again on her usual side of the bed, where Paul had been the last few nights, she looked across the room to the armchair by the window and thought about him saying he thought he had dreamt of someone sitting there wrapped in a rug watching over him, lit by tiny lights. Memories came flooding back, half-forgotten words and snippets of conversations. She blinked away tears when she thought of her joking that while he was ill, she had him in her power and how he replied, half asleep, "you always did". If this were a court case she would say there was conflicting evidence, and maybe he was attracted to her, but if the multi-dating gossip was true, then all those things he did and said, were normal for him, despite how significant they seemed to her.

Chapter 32

When Sofia opened the door to the reception area of her office on the Thursday morning, it felt as if she had been away for a month, as if she must re-familiarise herself with the place again. Five days and nights with Paul, she thought, and I seem to have moved into a changed reality, a bit like it felt at home last night after he left, as if I had been abandoned in a strange place. She gave herself a mental shake, said hi to Bayden and continued down the corridor to her room. Two hours later, after an hour of catching up with Clare, she was back in normal work mode. A couple of her jobs had been dealt with by others, client appointments had been re-scheduled, and she was soon over the feeling she had experienced when she first arrived.

'You're looking tired,' said Clare as she got up

and gathered up the files she had brought in. 'You're not coming down with whatever it was your patient had, are you? And how are they getting on, anyway?'

'Oh no, I'm fine,' said Sofia, and quickly considered how to respond to the questions, which would surely be repeated by others before the day was over. 'It was a distant cousin – he got the 'flu or something like it - it came over him like a tidal wave while we were having a catch-up dinner on Friday night. And he lives on his own, so I dragged him back to my place because we were only two blocks away. Lack of sleep is my worst problem – it was really full-on, around the clock nursing there for a couple of days and nights. But he's back at his place now, recovering.'

The questions about her health resurfaced in the lunchroom, when Stewart, the senior partner, came in just after Sofia had sat down with the sandwich she had bought on her way to work.

'Good to see you back! And congratulations on the funny little case about the fraudster and the motor home – Clare was telling us over lunch the other day how well it worked out in the end. Very satisfying.'

It made Sofia smile; the pleasure she got from what she always thought of as another 'happy ending' seemed to be a shared feeling.

'It was so nice for Mr Somerville. He's very old, and he'd been so worked up about the trial and being a witness. He's seen too many court dramas on TV, I think, and he was expecting to be grilled by the defence and lose track of what he was saying.'

'And another thing,' said Stewart and sat down beside her with his lunch in a plastic lunchbox with a picture of Roadrunner on the lid. 'Clare said you add notes to the client file when something like that happens, like the old guy loving the motorhome and deciding to live in it instead of selling it. When and why did you start doing that?'

Despite how friendly his tone of voice was, Sofia wondered if he was going to object to it, but she could see no possible reason why he would.

'I've done it nearly since I started here,' she said. 'There was an early case where I was defending a young guy, who had mugged a woman in a Lower Hutt carpark, a legal aid client. And then the victim, who had cried when she read out her victim impact statement in the courtroom and said how she had lost her faith in humanity, called me much later – very unexpectedly. She said someone had left an insulated bag on her back doorstep while she was at work, and inside were six little boxes of food ready for the freezer and a card from the mother of the mugger, saying how sorry she was, and that she hoped some nice home-made food would be a comfort.' She smiled to herself at the memory of that phone call. 'And the woman who called me, the victim, she said it really *did* make her feel better and she thought I should know. So, I called the mugger's mother and said I knew about the gift, and I thought it was a lovely gesture, and *she* in turn told me her son had asked her to do something because he felt bad having scared a woman so badly that she cried in court. So, I got the file out and added the story – and I've just continued since.'

'It's a lovely idea,' said Stewart, 'but do you really expect anyone to find those notes and read them?'

Sofia smiled. 'Oh no, not at all, but that's not the point – I just think of it as adding a little footnote to history. It only happens now and then, and I think it's worth writing it down. And then when it's done, Clare and I break out the secret box of chocolates from my filing cabinet and have a couple of chocolates each – those special ones with cherry brandy inside wrapped in red foil.' She laughed. 'Drinking on the job - I've just realised! But we see so many worried and furious and sometimes desolate people that celebrating something good feels nice.'

Stewart swallowed a mouthful of his lunch and looked at her as if he had never seen her before, part puzzled and part amazed. 'You have a wonderful way of dealing with your clients, I must say! You go that extra mile and then you invent a lovely way to celebrate the final, good outcome. I'm very proud of you!'

On her way back to her room, Sofia made a detour to talk to Clare and said in a whisper, 'Did you know that Stewart has a lunchbox with Roadrunner on the lid?'

Clare leaned across the desk and whispered back, 'Yes, his granddaughter gave it to him for his birthday and now he brings it every day – he's a good grandpa.'

That afternoon, before they locked everything up for the day, Sofia walked down the corridor to the archive room, located the file with her grandfather's name and added the separate envelope with the confession and the photo of the house in Trentham.

Chapter 33

S ofia stood on the pavement at a busy street corner, with muted chaos and stalled rush hour traffic all around her and called Clare at the office.

'Clare, I'll be late, maybe an hour? I'm a witness at a traffic accident, so I have to stay here for a little while.'

'God, you're not hurt again are you?'

A police officer turned up beside her with a notebook in her hand, and Sofia said quickly, 'No, I'm fine, but they want to talk to me now - I've got to go, see you soonish.'

She turned to the officer. 'Sorry, had to inform my workplace that I'll be late. Now what do you want first, name and contact details or what happened?'

'Name etc first,' said the woman and folded back

the cover of her notebook. 'And workplace number plus your cell phone number.'

'I'll give you my business card,' said Sofia and fished around in her bag. 'It's got most of what you need on it.'

A couple of minutes later they progressed to what Sofia had seen. 'I saw him grab the satchel, I was just behind him – he nearly knocked the man over, just ripped it from his shoulder, and then he took off across the street. The guy who'd been robbed ran after him, but he got hit by that red car over there, so I ran across the road and followed the thief.'

'OK, and then?'

'I caught up with him at the next corner, he ran straight into the side of a taxi. I saw it happening, he counted on the taxi continuing around the corner, so when it braked very suddenly he ran into it.' Recalling the scene, she started to laugh. 'And he tried to sidestep to the right in the last second, presumably to continue running around the back of the taxi, but his right foot caught against the rear wheel of the car – I think he broke his ankle. Talk about just deserts! So, I called 111 and obviously so did someone at this corner too. Your colleagues down there have the satchel now, so you can tell the owner it's safe. I only just got back here, so I haven't tried to talk to him yet.'

The officer grinned. 'What a tale! And well done for taking off after him. I'll coordinate with the guys on the corner. We'll be in touch about signing a statemen.'

'Is the guy who got hit badly hurt?'

'I don't know – he's in the back of the ambulance, conscious and I think he's broken his arm. Perhaps those two will end up side-by-side in ED.'

They looked at each other and laughed, and then Sofia started out for the office.

'What happened,' asked Clare. 'Did some idiot pedestrian walk out in front of a bus again?'

'No, but pretty exciting,' said Sofia. 'I must go to the restroom and clean my filthy knees - I've been kneeling on the wet street beside a robber. How about you make us each a coffee and I'll tell you what happened in my room in five.'

'OK,' said Clare to her retreating back. 'There's a parcel for you on your desk, a big one.'

'Oh my God, look at your knees!' said Clare when Sofia walked into her office and hung her suit jacket on the hook behind her door. 'I thought you said you knelt beside someone, but those looks like deep grazes. What did you wash them with?'

'Hand soap and paper towels,' said Sofia and sat down in her chair and hid her knees under her desk. 'It will be OK, Clare, it's not serious. I threw my tights in the bin and scrubbed the dirt out of the scratches pretty thoroughly. Where did this box come from?'

'Someone delivered it to Bayden this morning first thing – I've not idea what's in it. It's not that heavy compared to the size of the box, so it's probably something that's very carefully packaged.'

Sofia looked suspiciously at Clare, because she knew that look; Clare was trying hard not to laugh and only partially succeeding.

'Anyway,' said Clare. 'Tell me why your knees look like they do – what really happened?'

Telling the story took only a few minutes but when she was halfway through, Bayden knocked on her open door and came in. 'That sounds fascinating!' he said. 'I noticed your knees when you came in. Do you want to see the video?'

'Video? Of what?'

'Of you battling with a robber, it's on the Stuff website – I don't know how someone your size managed to keep that guy on the ground.'

'Oh, for God's sake, he'd broken his ankle – he

wasn't going anywhere, but when I knelt down to see how damaged he was, he got … agitated, let's say. It did become a bit of a wrestling match. But I got the bag off him. Hand that phone over, please.'

They clustered around Bayden's phone and watched the short video taken from behind Sofia as she runs full tilt down the street after the thief who is a few steps ahead of her, then he collides violently with the side of the taxi, falls to the ground and Sofia throws herself down beside him and grabs the bag.

'I just wanted to get the bag back,' she said and looked at the others. 'I didn't know he'd broken his ankle, so I thought he'd get up again and run off.'

'That explains the grazes,' said Clare and got up to take their cups back to the lunchroom. 'You practically slid along on your knees. I'm going to fetch the antiseptic cream from the first aid box – I don't like the thought of what horrible filth was on that street.'

When Clare put the tube of cream on the desk, Sofia had taken a call and was making notes while she talked, she gestured a thank you and went back to her note taking. Two calls later and a surprise visit from one of the partners to see how she was, and Sofia could finally open the box. On top of a lot of crumpled newspaper lay a card, a picture of Greytown in the eighteen hundreds, with horse-drawn carriages on the unpaved main street and ladies in long skirts and large hats on the sidewalk. On the back was just one sentence: "Words aren't enough to express how grateful I am. P"

She knew what was in the box without looking further; it had to be the Etling bowl – she poked her hand into the mass of scrunched up paper and felt the deeply sculpted bottom of the bowl. She remained standing with her head bowed at the low cupboard in the corner of her room where she had opened the box. She still had the scissors in one hand and the card in the other, and her eyes were full of tears. Trying to pull herself together before anyone came in, she blinked rapidly, put the card back in the box and closed the flaps. And now what? she thought. Now I must call him and say thank you, a text message won't do. I must get it just right, words and tone of voice, so I sound as pleased as I am, but if he asks to meet me, I must have a credible reason why I can't.

Still absorbed in her thoughts, Sofia didn't notice Clare coming back with a file in her hand. 'Oh, you've opened it – was I right? It's something breakable?'

'Yes, very precious,' said Sofia. 'A thank you present – nothing to do with work, a gift for something I did for a friend. What's that file?'

'It's a new client – she hasn't got a lawyer at all, she said she's never needed one before, and it's just your kind of thing. Do you remember Miss Sorenson last year or maybe the year before? The cat poisoning case? This one got your name from her. It's about damage to a rental property by a serial renter cum house wrecker. You'll find a brief summary in the file. She's coming in on Monday.'

And then the phone rang again, and Sofia picked it up and it was lunchtime before she had a moment to call Paul.

Sofia had to steel herself to make the call, and she was hoping it would go to voicemail so she wouldn't have to talk to him. Somehow the thought of turning down an invitation for coffee seemed beyond her, and she couldn't think what excuse or what words she would use. The conflict between wanting to see him and knowing she shouldn't, that it would only hurt her and that she must end this impossible friendship created a feeling of physical pain in her chest. How will I manage it, she thought, as she sat with the phone in her hand, how can I sound normal and not hurt him, but still turn him down?

'Hi,' he said when he heard who it was, when she

finally got her courage up to make the call. 'How are you?'

'More to the point, how are *you*?' she said. 'And thank you so much for the Etling bowl – a far too expensive thing to give me, but I will treasure it. How on earth did you get it here so fast? I was late in this morning, and they told me it arrived first thing.'

'I dropped it off on my way to work – I feel quite good now, so I thought I'd go back to work.'

'But how did you get it? Don't tell me you drove up there yesterday when you should have been resting!'

'Oh, I was fine by then, and the drive over that road was a great experience. We'll have to go to Greytown again – I found a café with an outdoor area out the back that had great food – I had lunch there. Would you like to go out for a meal or a drink this weekend?'

Inside her head a little voice shouted, "Yes! Yes!" but she schooled her voice to sound casual and slightly regretful. 'I can't – there's a case coming up next week that's so complicated and I'm spending all my time working on sorting out some of the evidence and discussing things with the QC whose case it is.'

To her surprise Paul didn't try to persuade her, he just asked which QC was involved, made a sympathetic comment when she told him who it was, and said he would ask her again the following weekend.

Mixed messages, thought Sofia, when they had said goodbye and sat for a moment staring down at the phone. I think I'm right about what this is all about; he has one or more other women and what he feels for me is just friendship and gratitude. If he was in any way serious he would surely have protested or tried to persuade me. In her mind, the conversation had removed the ambiguity of their situation. He did not want a romantic of sexual relationship with her, he just wanted them to be friends, and that was not possible. In her mind she could see the scene play out as if it had already happened, when something she said, or did, revealed that she was in love with him and how he might react. The mere thought of it made her cringe. Would the expression on his face be pity or embarrassment? Either way it wasn't something she could risk. Loving someone who didn't love her was one thing, something painful she could hold close to her heart and never expose to the world, but for him to find out was too humiliating to contemplate.

Chapter 34

Sofia got home after walking up Mt Victoria to the Byrd memorial and getting pummelled by a strong south-westerly wind, eager for a hot drink and something to eat. Somehow a lonely ramble in challenging weather had seemed a suitably melancholy thing to do, but now she just felt that she had wasted a morning and not in any way made herself feel better. But she had no sooner hung her storm jacket up in the hall than Bitsy rang the doorbell.

'I know it's Saturday,' she said. 'And mum said I mustn't bother you in the weekend, and I don't want to come in, I just want to give you this for Paul.'

She held out a folded paper with a paperclip holding it together and turned to go.

"Wait!' said Sofia. 'I'd love some company. Why

don't you check with your mum if it's OK that you have lunch with me?'

Half an hour later Bitsy sat on a stool at the breakfast counter watching Sofia making toast fingers to go with their soft-boiled eggs. 'Why are you cutting the toast like that? It looks like food for dolls to eat.'

'It's so you can dip them into the egg yolk when you've knocked the top off your boiled egg – it's a lovely way to eat eggs. My French grandmother always did this for me when I was a little girl.'

'What's she called?'

'I call her grand-mere – she lives in a little town outside Paris, and she has a dog called Pierrot, a little white fluffy dog who barks like crazy every time someone knocks on the door.'

'I would like a little dog,' said Bitsy wistfully, 'but mum says not until I'm bigger and can take it for walks on my own. Maybe when I'm ten or eleven.'

Sofia's phone signalled a message and Bitsy picked it up. 'It's from Marcus,' she said. 'It starts with "is there no end to the drama …" – I wonder what it means.'

Sofia left the message for later and sat down beside Bitsy to show her how to dip her toast fingers in the egg.

'This is fun,' said Bitsy when she had finished. 'I

like how the eggs gets emptier and emptier – and then you eat the white part last. You're very clever. It's a bit drippy, but I like it. Can we read that message now? What does drama mean?'

She handed Sofia the phone and watched while she unlocked it. 'You'll have to teach me how to do that,' she said.

'Not for another three or four years,' said Sofia, thinking with horror of what Bitsy could achieve if she knew how to get into the phone any time she fancied. 'About the same time as you get your dog, probably. Oh, I see – Marcus saw something on the internet and it's dramatic, which means it's exciting or scary.'

'Read me the whole thing, please,' said Bitsy. 'I like to know what's going on. I always read my mum's messages on her phone but they're boring, not like yours. Hers are mostly about work or from dad.'

For a brief moment Sofia's mind failed to provide the explanation and then she nearly laughed. Of course, Bitsy read her messages, just like she changed the ring tones when she was supposedly playing Blockheads on Sofia's phone as a reward. I didn't factor in how clever and inquisitive she is, thought Sofia, I must be a bit more careful. She's probably searched through all my social media apps as well. Thank heavens she doesn't seem to have posted anything crazy – or not that I've noticed anyway.

'Ok, this is the whole message: "Is there no end to the drama in your life? Just saw the video of you giving chase in great style and in high heels, particularly liked the way you wrestled the bag off the guy. Hope you're not injured?'

'Show me the video!' demanded Bitsy. 'I want to see some drama. I like scary things.'

Sofia followed the link in Marcus's text message and passed the phone to Bitsy, who sat mesmerised watching Sofia run down the street after a man with bag. 'It's you! You got him! What did he do?'

'He stole that bag from a man, who started running after him and got hit by a car. So, when he fell over, I ran after the thief, and *he* ran into a car as well! He thought the car would continue around the corner, but it stopped, so he ran full tilt into it. That's what drama means, the perfect illustration.'

'Served him right!' said Bitsy vengefully. 'The thief, I mean – that he ran into a car too. I hope he broke something, and it hurt. What happened next? Any more drama?'

'No, nothing dramatic at all. I just had to talk to the police and tell them what had happened and then I went to work with my filthy, grazed knees.'

This explanation seemed to satisfy Bitsy, who

handed the phone back and said, 'Would you like to see my note that I did for Paul? I really like him – it's not a note, it's more like a drawing with words.'

She picked up the folded paper from the bench and handed it to Sofia and watched her carefully while she studied the drawing.

'I think it's the best one you've ever done – and such good writing too. I'll give it to him next time I see him.'

There was no point offering Bitsy the opportunity to hand it to Paul herself, because she would never see him again. At some stage, I must invent an excuse for his absence that she can understand, thought Sofia, and tell her he said he really liked it. The things we do to protect those we love from disappointment! Who would have thought I'd acquire a small friend, who would get involved in my life to this degree, and in addition form such a liking for a man I am removing from my life?

When Bitsy left to go home, Sofia unfolded the paper and studied the drawing again. A table, slightly out of perspective, with three people sitting around it, huge mugs on the table and an open book hovering in the air above it. One very small person with black hair, one medium sized person with brown hair in a ponytail, and one huge person opposite them. Above their heads Bitsy had written their names with long arrows angling out. Sofia laughed to herself at how large Bitsy had made Paul and thought he must have made a real impression, perhaps she could feel that strength and kindness she herself experienced when she was with him. At the bottom of the drawing, she had written "To my ~~freiend~~ friend Paul who told me a funny hen story."

Over the next few days, a steady stream of attention came Sofia's way, not only due to her friends sharing the chase video on social media, but also, she suspected, due to Bayden's open admiration for how she had chased the bag thief. She should have been able to predict it, but his efforts to spread her fame resulted in too much social media attention and far too many interruptions at work. Since the various out-of-character events that had taken place in the last few weeks, Bayden now regarded her very differently from the slightly bored disdain she had merited before. Now, when Sofia pushed open the tall glass door from the lift foyer into the office, Bayden would look up with a smile and greet her with affection and as much pride as if he had created her himself.

Margot's call arrived when Sofia was staring out the window, frustrated and mentally cursing the impulse that had made her offer to take care of a case for a colleague who was on a month's leave. Not that the case itself was complicated or unusual, but his notes were nearly illegible. She had just hit on the idea to ask his secretary for help, but as she got up her phone buzzed.

'Hi,' said Margot cheerfully. 'Aren't you just the best! I've just seen that video of you running down the street in high heels in hot pursuit of a thief – well done!'

'Ha!' said Sofia, who felt as if she was on a recorded loop. 'Nothing great about having my poor knees grazed and bleeding and the toes my favourite shoes seriously scuffed. But satisfying, all the same.'

Margot laughed, 'A small price to pay for being a heroine, perhaps. And also satisfying that the thief broke his ankle or leg or whatever it was – just deserts, as they say. Have you got time for lunch this week?'

Sofia hesitated between her unexpected feeling of wanting to see Margot again, and the self-protective urge to stay away from situations where her feeling of loss and low mood might become obvious and require explanations.

'I'm sorry, but I just can't take lunch hours this week – I'm just having a five minute sandwich in the office lunchroom. One of the guys here, is away on unexpected leave and I'm covering some of his clients and cases, so my days are full-on. How about I call you when things are a bit quieter – I'd love to have lunch and not feel rushed.'

A few minutes later, Sofia stood beside Nora's desk while she studied the illegible notes with a frown just as Sofia had done.

'For God's sake!' she exclaimed and turned another page. 'This is the worst scribble I've ever seen. Ben's got terrible handwriting, but this lot looks as if he wrote it in the dark and half asleep. Leave it with me and I'll sort it out for you. When do you need it back?'

'At the end of the week will be fine, thanks.'

By the time Clare was ready to leave, Sofia had made progress with two urgent cases and was reading the typed notes Nora had already forwarded, amazed at how helpful they were, clear and concise now that she could read them.

'You're a genius! Many thanks!' she replied to Nora's email and returned to the case she was working on for one of her own clients.

'Busy?' asked Clare from the open door. 'Do you have time to sign a few things before I go, or should I leave them until tomorrow?'

'Is it five already? I've been so flat out today I haven't really noticed the time. No, I'll sign them now and then they're out of the way.'

Sofia noticed the searching look Clare gave her as she turned in the door but ignored it, reluctant to have to respond to whatever questions Clare might want to ask.

Gradually the background noise of the office, the sounds that normally formed a nearly unnoticeable backdrop, ceased and when Stewart looked in, she had worked for a couple of hours since Clare left. When he spoke, she looked up with a feeling of dislocation, suddenly noticed the total silence and uncertain of what time it was.

'You're working late – did Ben leave too much of his stuff to you?'

'No, don't worry – once Nora had deciphered the hieroglyphics he left me it's all good. I'm just preparing for the trial tomorrow. I'll set the alarm when I leave.'

Having a heavy workload was a blessing in disguise. Sofia worked late into the evenings, either at the office or at home, and had little time to think of her own problems. She only went to bed when she was too exhausted to keep her eyes open, and gradually her tiredness built up and added to her low mood. She went to work very early each morning and had started eating her lunch at her desk to avoid being in the staff lunchroom and having to talk to colleagues. Clare provided cups of coffee at intervals and in a departure from her normal inquisitiveness refrained from asking questions.

The case of the key scratcher, whom she was defending in court, was over in two hours, after a surprising new witness provided a detailed description of the accused walking slowly past her house and running his key along the side of six cars parked on the street. Not only was Miss Drummond's evidence clear and unhesitating, but the video recorded by her Ring doorbell was in itself enough to bring in a verdict of guilty whatever else cropped up. After a whispered conference with her client Sofia got up and announced that the accused wished to change his plea to guilty.

If only we had more people like Miss Drummond, thought Sofia after she had said goodbye to her client, and if they all had that kind of doorbell, life would be so much easier. The sentencing was scheduled for December, and she felt fairly certain that her client would not be let off lightly. The neighbourhood had seen many incidents of expensive cars being keyed in the last few weeks before her client was caught and she felt fairly sure it was a habit of his.

She was hurrying towards the entrance to the courthouse, checking her phone as she went and thinking she would be able to fit in at least three hours work before her next client appointment at half past four, when a familiar voice called out, 'Sofia! Wait!' She came to an abrupt halt and felt her chest constrict as if she would not be able to draw her next breath.

'Paul - hi!' she said and tried desperately to make her voice casual and cheerful 'How are you?'

'I'm just fine.' He studied her face and slowly his expression changed to a puzzled frown. 'But how are you? You look exhausted, are you OK?'

'Just seriously overworked with a bit too much on my plate right now – one of the guys at work is unexpectedly off for four weeks and I've taken on a lot of his stuff. I've been doing extra hours both in the office and at home lately and probably not getting enough sleep.'

'No time for dinner?' His face was neutral now, his voice casual and she knew he had picked up on her first reaction when he called out her name. Her instinctive urge to flee had probably manifested itself in some kind of involuntary movement, and now he was being careful and possibly confused.

'I can't,' said Sofia and managed to produce a smile. 'I really can't do anything but work, eat and sleep until the worst is over. When people have to take long leave with no warning there's so much on the go – you know how it is.'

'Well, look after yourself,' he said. 'I'll call you in a couple of weeks and see how you're going. I was nice to see you.'

As he turned to go, her hand still holding the phone reached out as if to hold him back and he must have caught the movement out of the corner of his eye, because he swung around. 'Yes?'

'Oh, nothing,' she said and heard her voice wobble. 'Sorry, I really must go.' She turned and headed back into the large foyer, desperate to get away before the tears that pooled in her eyes overflowed.

'It's such a nasty way of ruining things for others with no gain for yourself,' said Clare when Sofia returned just after lunch and told her the outcome of the key scratcher case. 'It's as if they feel a need to punish others for having what they themselves can't afford.'

'I know – it's depressing at times. When I talked to this guy, when I took it as a *pro bono* case, I nearly asked him why he did it. I don't normally do that, but just this once I really wanted to know. And then today after he changed his plea to guilty and it was over, he told me it was a dare, some kind of TikTok challenge – he was looking for fame and recognition. Well, he didn't say that, but it was clearly what motivated him. It's like those ramraids where they film themselves and put it online. I did ask if he had a mate standing around filming him, and he said no - but I didn't believe him.'

'That QC you're working with, what's his name? Smithers – his secretary called and said to tell you the prosecutor has asked for the case to be postponed due to some new evidence they've found. He'll be in touch when he knows more.'

That evening, Sofia was unable to concentrate either on work or reading. Her mind repeatedly played back the short conversation with Paul and the look on his face; it had made her feel dreadful to be so dismissive, when she had wanted to take hold of his arm and say, 'Let's go and have coffee.'

She could picture him sitting opposite her that night not long ago, when he told her about his wife's affair and the baby. She remembered how they had looked at each other across the coffee table and both known that they totally trusted each other. And now she had brushed him off, made him feel that she was not his friend. Perhaps he wouldn't call her, just write their friendship off and forget about her. That last thought tipped her over the edge, and she cried, devastated that she had hurt him and unable to see any way of undoing the damage without causing herself more agony.

Chapter 36

By Saturday morning Sofia felt she had regained some of her inner balance after spending a couple of hours the previous night sitting in her nearly dark bedroom with only the bud-lights on the windowsill providing light. She sat in the little blue armchair, closed her eyes and allowed her mind to drift. She had not done it deliberately, not anticipated that it would give her peace, but after a while she felt as if she was back to the time of Paul's illness, and if she opened her eyes she would see him sleeping in her bed, and though she knew he wasn't there, it calmed her.

Her conflicted emotions and the pain she felt were tempered by remembering him there, the feel of her hand on his cheek to calm him, how she had smoothed the lip balm on his bottom lip and the feeling of her hand holding his wet wrist to stop him trying to push her away in the shower. She could delve into the past, re-live what she had done and said, and nearly imagine the smell of his hot skin, the feel of the stubble on his cheek. When she finally went to bed, she didn't cry but lay quietly looking at the bud-lights, resigning herself to living with this sense of loss which she knew would be with her day and night for a long time.

She woke up early the next morning, feeling unrested and tired still. Accept your fate, she told herself briskly, still speaking out loud, don't rage against it, take it into your heart and just live with it, let it become part of you or it will destroy you.

She thought of what a university friend had said once when her boyfriend had abruptly broken up with her. She had told Sofia that the only way she could go to sleep without crying was to put her headset on and play they music they often played in the car. 'It's like a shadow of the past,' she said. 'It gives me a little bit of the feeling of what it was like when we were together.' At the time it had meant nothing to Sofia, but now she recalled the comment and thought how closely it fitted what she had experienced the previous evening.

When a message from Paul popped up on her phone she very nearly didn't open it but delaying things would not help her. She pressed the message icon, and it was exactly what she had thought it would be: "I would like to meet you today, however briefly. Something is wrong and I need to understand what caused it."

Formulating a credible and un-dismissive way of saying she couldn't or wouldn't meet him, but without hurting him, seemed too hard to work out, but after putting it off for half an hour, she forced herself to reason through the options. Standing inside the balcony doors vacantly looking out at the streetscape, she defined the most relevant things.

She had to delay meeting with him until she felt sure she could handle it and not be left floundering, stumbling over words or worse, in tears. At the same time, she didn't want to hurt him or be dismissive, but finding a middle ground seemed impossible just then, and she opted for the simple but cowardly way out and replied: "Two online meetings this morning re court case next week and new evidence. Meeting with old friend this afternoon. Tomorrow morning?" Putting it off would not make it any easier, but she felt exhausted already from worry and indecision.

Unable to wait for his answer, not wanting to see what he said, she sent a quick message to

Helen, asking to meet her after lunch "for a coffee or a drink, timing up to you, please call me on landline" and turned her phone right off. Fully aware that this was a ridiculous thing to do, she still did it, because it meant she could delay reading Paul's reply, or worse, having to take a call from him.

I've never given him my landline number, she thought, and it's not listed, it gives me a bit of space to work out what I'm going to say to him.

When the phone on the kitchen bench rang she still hesitated to pick it up, her breath caught in her throat as she tried to imagine how she would respond if it was Paul.

'What's this about calling on the landline?' said Helen. 'You just sent me a text, for God's sake – what's going on?'

'I've turned my phone off – someone is hounding me, and I simply don't want to hear the alerts or see the messages today, so I'm turning it off for a few hours. Have you got time to meet?'

"I'd love to, I'm on my own and I've got nothing to do this afternoon, unless I get super energetic and start cleaning the flat - so how about we have lunch at Prefab. I know you haven't been there, not unless you went after last time we talked, but I love it! Sorry, have to go, the courier is at the door. I'll meet you there at half past twelve, you can tell me then what this mystery is about.'

At twenty to one, Sofia sat down at a corner table at Prefab, admired the décor and the setting, and prepared to endure an interrogation from Helen, who would insist on finding out every detail about the turned-off phone and who was harassing her. But when Helen entered, Paul and a tall, slim woman with blond hair came in nearly directly behind her and Sofia turned her head down and looked at the menu without taking in the words, desperately hoping that Paul would not look her way.

Helen sat down at the table and gave Sofia's shoulder a little push. 'What are you so engrossed in? Starving?'

'Sorry, I think I have to leave.' Sofia's voice was barely audible. 'I can't stay here, let's go – right now!'

And then fate decided to tweak the thumbscrews one turn more, and Paul appeared in front of her.

'I must go now,' Sofia said and pushed her chair back, and without looking at either Paul or Helen, she walked out the door and ran crossed the street. Behind her she heard Helen's voice calling out, 'Wait for me, Sofia!'

Sofia stopped until Helen caught up with her. 'What on earth is going on? Why did you leave like that? Oh no, you're crying!'

Helen put her arms around Sofia's shoulder and moved her to the inner side of the pavement. 'What's wrong? What happened back there?'

Sofia was sobbing and wiping her face with her hands and when she looked up she realised that Helen had turned her around and now she was facing the café across the street, and she moaned. 'Please let's walk away from here, I don't want him to see me like this. Let's just go!'

She slid out from under Helen's arm and started walking fast without checking if Helen followed. She felt desperate, as if the only thing that mattered was getting further away from the café. Helen appeared beside her and said, 'Let's go to my place – I'm not letting you go home in this state and you're going in the wrong direction, anyway. Come on, we'll just walk together, no need to talk.'

The walk to Helen and Oscar's place took twenty minutes and neither of them said a single word on the way.

Chapter 37

Helen turned from the espresso machine and handed Sofia a mug. 'Now, you must tell me what this is all about. I haven't seen you cry since you were nine or ten and sprained your ankle playing bullrush at school. What's that bloody man done to you?'

Tears once again spilled over and rolled down Sofia's cheeks. She put the cup on the kitchen counter and wiped her face with her hands, and Helen took a step closer and wrapped her arms around her.

'Oh, darling, please don't start crying again.' She rocked Sofia gently. 'It can't be that bad, surely not! Did he hurt you? Did he say something nasty about you? Or is he stalking you? You must tell me what he did, or I can't help you.'

'He didn't do anything – and nobody can help me,' said Sofia into Helen's shoulder. 'It's too late now, it's hopeless. I wish I'd never met him.'

'Come and sit down and we'll just wait a while until you've calmed down a bit and then you'll be able to tell me.' Helen let her go, picked up both mugs and led the way to the living room. 'Here,' she said and motioned to the sofa. 'Sit here with me – maybe it will be easier to tell me what this is about if you don't have to look at me while you talk. And you can cry as much as you like, we have plenty of tissues.'

Sofia sat down, wiped her eyes with her fingers again, and sniffled. 'It's so hard to talk about it,' she said, her voice thick with tears. 'And you won't understand - I hardly understand it myself. I've never felt like this in my life.'

'Try me!' said Helen and put a tissue in her hand. 'I don't think I've ever failed to understand you – sometimes I think I'm the only one who really does. I know why you've never had a long-term relationship after that controlling troll you were with a few years ago, and because you're so good at concealing things most people have no idea how that affected you.' She paused for a moment, as if hesitating, then continued. 'They only see the top student and the serious, career driven person you are, not the girl inside who never believed it when we told her how cute and clever she was. You always thought you were not enough of *anything* – first thanks to your mother and then that damn ex-partner of yours! It makes me furious on your behalf!'

Sofia said nothing, but she wiped her eyes properly, reached for another tissue and blew her nose. 'I know,' she said finally, sitting up straighter. 'I've known it for some time. I always felt inadequate, like I was just pretending to be capable and clever, like I fooled everyone. Inside I knew I was pretty useless at most things, and it was as if I was expecting to be unmasked at any moment, found to be inadequate. But just recently I've realised I'm not like that, and I know there are things I'm good at – I mean, I really *do* believe I'm good at a lot of things now.'

'Impostor syndrome,' said Helen. 'You are – or were - the perfect example. But I interrupted you, sorry, do carry on, tell me how this happened, what made you realise.'

'It's so complicated because I fell in love with the person who somehow gave me the confidence to realise I'm not an impostor, and now I think of him all the time and I want to be with him. But that's not why I love him, I fell in love before he had kind of snapped me out of how I felt about myself. You see, he told me such surprising things, like how he used to sit in on trials I was in, just short bits here and there and sometimes he actually tried to be there for the closing argument, he said I was so good at it. And some other things too, and since he told me those things I've felt myself changing – it's been amazing. It's like things make more sense when he says them, different from anyone else telling me things.'

She could sense Helen's attention becoming intense, but she said nothing, so Sofia continued. 'And it's not just that he's changed how I think of myself, it's far more than that. Like when he fixed my finger in that café and he was so kind, and I knew he was really special and every time he touched me, I just wanted him not to let go. It's something strange, Helen. It's like there's some kind of … maybe an aura around him, it's like a warmth or a strength that just wraps itself around you.'

Sofia turned her head to look directly at Helen and tried to smile at herself. 'I sound like an absolute twit – like someone in a soppy novel, but I had no idea anyone could make you feel like that. So, I fell in love with him nearly on the spot. But now that I know he's already got other interests – or one at least - I can't be his friend, it's too painful and it makes me so miserable. I know my case is hopeless, I know he doesn't love me. So, when I saw him just now in the bistro with that woman and he came over and was so nice, it just broke my heart.' She took a deep breath to steady herself.

'Oh shit!' said Helen finally after a short pause. 'And I thought he'd done something terrible to you and I was ready to go and find him to tell him what I think of him – how absurd! But I don't get it – this thing about it being hopeless. Why is it necessarily hopeless? For heaven's sake, just go for it, seduce him or something. And what do you mean by other interests? Other women? Or men?'

Sofia blew her nose again, took a sip of her cooling coffee and tried to decide how to start. Somehow all the various factors that had brought her to this point and to this state of despair, were nearly too complex to unravel so somebody else would understand. After a few moments, while Helen again sat silent beside her, she said, 'I'll have to tell you the whole story right from the beginning, I think, and it's such a long story and I don't want to sit here like a damp blob of misery if Oscar walks in.'

'Oscar is away for the weekend with the school football team, he's taken over as coach this term, and they won't even be back at the school until five pm tomorrow, so don't worry about him – take as long as you like. You stay here and drink your coffee,' said Helen and got to her feet. 'I must go to the bathroom, and I'll bring a damp facecloth back for your poor blotchy face.'

Chapter 38

Helen she returned and handed a cold, wet facecloth to Sofia. 'I'm not moving off this sofa until you've told me the whole thing, so I understand what caused this melt-down,' she said.

From the dislocated finger to the date with Paul over coffee, Sofia told the story all while folding and refolding the wet cloth. She listed every single feeling she had experienced, Paul's words and actions and her own thoughts and reactions. Describing what she overheard over her café brunch, when the woman at the next table told her companion about Paul's lover, the elegant, blond woman, nearly reduced her to tears again.

'Because when I found out he was in love with someone else, or maybe having an affair with somebody else, and that gossipy woman said she thought he multi-dated, that's the word she used - then I knew I wouldn't have a chance. I think he wanted to introduce met to that woman back there – the blond woman he came in with. I've misread all those little gestures and the things he said, because I wanted them to be true, but that was just him being affectionate, like with a close friend. He doesn't feel for me what I feel for him.'

Helen sat silent holding her mug of untouched coffee in both hands and waited. Sofia glanced at her again, but there was no comment forthcoming, so she continued. 'But I gave in to temptation to see him, thinking we could be friends, that it would be enough, so when he asked me out for dinner I said yes. And he got so ill over dinner and that's what tipped me over the edge. Over the next few days and nights, I realised how much I love him, totally love him and I don't think I can stop, Helen! I've never felt like this before about anyone, it's agonising, sometimes when I think about it, I can't breathe properly.'

'Tell me what happened – I don't understand this thing about the dinner. Did he get ill in the restaurant? And how did it make you realise you love him?'

The story of those days and nights of looking after Paul, all that happened and all that had gone through her mind, took Sofia a long time to tell, because at times the emotions it brought to the surface nearly overwhelmed her. When she got to the point where she walked into the bedroom and thought Paul had died, she could hardly get the words out.

'Oh, Helen,' she said, and her voice was desolate. 'That's when I knew I'll never be the same again. I know he *didn't* die, but it kind of made me see how bleak my life would be if I couldn't be with him. I was such a fool, so *stupid* – I thought being good friends would be enough. At least I'd be able to see him now and then. But of course, it won't be enough, it would be torment to be with him when I know he loves someone else – I'd rather never see him again.'

The rest of the story was easier to tell, and she withheld nothing apart from what Paul had told her about his wife's affair and the baby, and her grandfather's confession.

'What an amazing story! It's the most dramatic and romantic falling in love story I've ever heard of in real life. But you can't give up! This is worth fighting for, or it's going to affect the rest of your life.'

'I know, Helen! I know I should kind of fight for him, but how do you do that? I don't think I can, because it would involve continuing to see him as a friend – and I simply can't do it! And you can't make somebody love you. Eventually I'd be bound to show that I love him – and he would either be embarrassed or pity me! I couldn't bear it, so now I'll have to learn how to control how I feel when I think of him, to keep my emotions under control and try to just soldier on.'

She turned sideways on the sofa and took Helene's hand and tried to smile. 'You are so kind, you're the best friend anyone could ever have, and I know I'm lucky to have you. I know you want to help me, but you must understand that some things aren't fixable, and this is one of them - there's nothing anyone can do, I just have to live with it.'

When she finally left Helen's place, after two glasses of wine and some cheese and crackers, she took a taxi home. Walking seemed beyond her, all she wanted was to get back home as fast as she could and to go to bed and try to sleep. A text from Paul was on her phone when she turned it on again in the car. "What's wrong? What did I say or do? Please call me! P"

She turned the phone off without responding

and stared out the window. All those people, she thought, look at them, out for a nice evening, and they don't know I'm inside this taxi feeling as if I have no future, miserable. Then she shook her head at how self-pitying that was and told herself to stop being so pathetic and get used to it.

Chapter 39

T he intercom from the street door, mounted on the wall in the kitchen, buzzed at lunchtime on Sunday and for a couple of moments she thought of not responding, pretending she was out. It was a dull morning with scudding clouds and a blustery wind, weather that suited her bleak mood.

Since she glanced at her phone when she woke up and then muted it, she hadn't looked at it again. Burying herself in work seemed to be the only thing that could take her mind off her emotions, and by half past eleven she had covered an impressive amount of preparation for the meeting she was due to attend with the QC the next afternoon to go through the new evidence. Typing up her handwritten notes took ages, but it was a great way to cement facts into her mind, ready to be pulled out later. Recording them and a getting Clare to type them into a Word document did not have the same lasting effect, and she wondered if she was the only lawyer in her firm to do it this way. It's actually a good thing this is such a complicated case, she thought, looking out at the dramatic sky, because I have to really concentrate. So many angles and seemingly contradictory pieces of evidence and all of them important. At least it's shown me how to keep all this inner turmoil at bay – work, lots of it, and the more complex and difficult it is, the better.

But in the end, after several buzzes from the intercom, she got sick of the sound and pressed the Talk button, and Paul's slightly distorted voice emerged. 'Would you please let me in, Sofia – we need to talk.'

'I'd rather not,' she said and waited.

'Well, I would rather you did,' said Paul calmly. 'If you don't press that button, I'll just stand here until someone goes in or out and sneak in behind them, and that might be a while on a Sunday – and it's damn cold out here. I need to talk to you, Sofia.'

'But I don't want to talk to you,' she said, trembling at how horrible it made her feel to have to say that to him.

'Why don't you want to talk to me?'

She could think of nothing to say, and he asked again, 'Why, Sofia?'

'I don't think you're good for me.' It was the only way she could put it, because saying she didn't like him or didn't trust him would have been a lie and hurtful. and she didn't want to hurt him.

'We can't have this conversation over the intercom,' said Paul, still sounding calm and reasonable. 'And I'll stay here all night if I have to – I mean that, Sofia! This is important and I want to talk to you.'

'OK,' was all she said, knowing he probably would stand there forever and get chilled and then he'd get in behind someone else and come and knock on her door. I'll just have to do it, she thought, I must deal with him somehow without letting him see how I feel about him, and then he'll go away.

She pressed the button and went to open her front door, but she didn't wait in the hall, instead she returned to the sitting room and stood with her back to the balcony door as if indicating there must be a physical distance between them.

She heard the front door close and then he was there, back in her flat where so much had changed for her, and she didn't greet him, she just remained where she was and waited.

'I'd like you to put a jacket on and come with

me,' he said, still calm and sounding as if nothing unusual was taking place. 'We'll go to my place.'

'I don't want to go to your place. Why would we go there?'

'There is something I need to show you – talking won't do it, I realise that now, and I would rather show you at my place than here. I think a new environment might help and it's not a conversation we can have in a public place. If you come with me, you might find we can talk.'

She tried to figure out what he meant, why it would be necessary to go to his house, and what it could possibly be that he wanted to show her. She knew he meant it, just as she knew he would never harm her, and that he wasn't dangerous, but it was too strange an idea to get her head around. So instead of continuing to protest, she said tiredly, 'OK.'

When he chuckled and said, 'Good girl!' the way he had done when he was fixing her finger, the memory nearly made her cry. She clenched her teeth and swallowed the feeling, picked up her phone from the table and walked ahead of him to the hall, put a jacket on, took her keys and opened the front door.

Neither of them said a single word while they walked to his car or on the drive to Island Bay. Later she would recall this strange, silent journey full of unspoken emotions and wonder how they managed it. At one point he reached across and without saying anything he put his hand on top of hers, and once more that ripple of warmth seemed to flow up her arm. She never took her eyes off the street ahead, her mind was in a strange state of limbo, she sat relaxed, nearly fatalistic, thinking that she must go through with whatever it was he wanted and then leave, and that would be the end of it.

Chapter 40

P aul's house was up high with a view over Island Bay, a very modern house which was a surprise and even in her weirdly detached state of mind at the time, Sofia registered the fact and wondered what she had expected; certainly not this, though she couldn't think why. Inside they went up a wide, curved staircase to a light and bright room with a wall of glass looking out over the stormy sea and the foam-capped waves.

Paul held his hand out. 'Can I take your jacket? And would you please sit down? And just so you know, this isn't the house I lived in with my wife.'

Without a word she shrugged out of her jacket, handed it to him and sat down.

'Now,' said Paul and got his phone out. He still sounded calm and relaxed. 'This is the phone I've had for nearly three years and it's the only one I have.' He held it out. 'Please take it and feel free to open any of the apps I use for talking to people, whether by text or by voice, look as far back as you like, open my Contacts folder and check who's there. I can promise I've deleted nothing, not a single text or any other kind of message. I'm going to make us lunch – take as long as you like.'

'I'd rather not,' said Sofia and didn't take the phone he was holding out towards her. The situation made her feel as if she was in some kind of art movie, the kind where nobody ever explains anything, and random things simply happen. 'I don't understand why you want me to do this.'

He sat down beside her, took her hand and put the phone into it, closed her fingers around it and got up again. 'Because I know what you've heard about me, and I want to prove it's nonsense. You'll find the person that you heard was my lover under the name Ursula in the contacts list - she's my first cousin and we're very fond of each other, we practically grew up together, so she's like a sister. She's recently returned to live in Wellington after spending nearly twenty years in Denmark, and we've been out together several times, catching up – on our own and with other people she knows. You're welcome to call her if you want to. I've no idea why this silly rumour started, but I can assure you I don't have a lover. In fact, I haven't dated anyone since my wife died. And the only way I can prove it to you is to give you access to everything, including my emails. Which will be easier on the laptop.' He pointed to dining table at one side of the room. 'Take as long as you like until you feel certain I'm telling the truth.'

She looked at him then, directly at him, for the first time since they left her flat. She opened her mouth to speak, then hesitated and said nothing, and he looked back showing no particular emotion, just waited.

She put the phone on the little table beside her. 'How do you know what I heard?' But even as she said the words, she knew.

'Helen told me. She's very worried about you. She called last night and said she wanted to know if the rumour was true.'

'What else did she say?' In her mind she lined up the things Helen knew about her, the damaging things her mother used to say when she was a teenager, the controlling tactics of her ex-partner that nearly broke her confidence, and she didn't know how she would feel about it if Paul heard these things from somebody else.

'She only said she needed to know, because that was probably the crucial reason you have decided you we can't be friends. But if that *isn't* the reason, then I need to understand what I might have said or done that made you feel that way.'

Sofia felt as if her mind had come to a standstill; she had no idea what to say or how she could explain anything without exposing herself to pity and be at a disadvantage. There is no way out, she thought, I can't explain it without revealing I've fallen in love with him. He wants us to be friends and I simply can't, there's no way forward.

She felt the silence like a physical presence and sat mute while he continued to patiently wait for her answer. Then suddenly she was desperate to get out of the house, she could not endure this tension a moment longer. She leapt to her feet and said, 'Let me go home - please!'

'Not yet - I thought you and I could tell each other anything, Sofia. Remember the things we told each other the other night? Things we had never told anyone else. Do you remember what you said when you thought I had died? You said, "Don't do this to me, I need you!" and you cried.'

For a moment Sofia closed her eyes, gathered up her last remnants of composure and said quietly, 'It's because I love you that I can't just be friends with you – it's too hard, I just can't do it.'

'I love you, too,' he said without moving closer.

'But I was worried it wouldn't work - I'm too old for you.'

'What? How could you be too old for me if you love me? What a ridiculous thing to say!' Suddenly she was angry and energized, felt as if she had walked through a door into a suddenly bright world. This was nonsense and she threw him a challenging glance. 'That's crazy – there must be another reason that you're not telling me. And how old *are* you anyway?'

'Remember that I've done this before,' he said. 'I married someone much younger than myself, and you know what came of that! I'm forty-three, and the gap is too wide. Or perhaps it isn't the age gap I should worry about, it's the kind of person I am that's the problem. I think my wife got bored with me for not only being more than a decade older than her, but also for not being exciting enough, not interested in most of the things that she filled her life with, too quiet - and that was the reason she had an affair. And the rest is history.'

'Oh, how *could* you put me through all this agony and not even *talk* to me about it!' Sofia exclaimed without moving towards him, outraged and furious. 'You're not too old, ten years is nothing, *nothing*! There are thousands of couples who have much bigger age gaps than that.'

'OK, maybe I'm not too old, but I'm too serious, I'm not interested in what's trendy or what people say on social media or gossip about famous people. I don't care about that aspect of life, I'm a very private person – I'm a premature fossil.'

'Oh, for God's sake!' she exclaimed and now she felt strong, more like herself than she had felt for ages. 'You're the least boring person I know, you're so cool and together – and so strong. I love you just the way you are, or perhaps I love you *because* of the way you are. I've never known anyone like you, not ever!'

She took three rapid steps towards him, closed the gap between them until she was so close she could feel the heat from his body through his clothes. Half laughing and half crying, she said, as if this was the clinching argument. 'And I love your hands!'

Ten minutes later they were still standing in the same spot in the middle of the room, and Paul slightly loosened his grip and held her away from him with his hands on her shoulders. 'I'm sorry I didn't talk to you about this earlier. I can see now it was stupid - and I can't explain why I didn't, but I kind of felt I was protecting myself and you, too.'

'God, how I wish you'd told me earlier! It would have saved so much agony. I think I started falling in love with you when you put my finger back in place and then there were moments, things you said and did, that made me think you had feelings for me too, but it you never said anything. So then I thought maybe those things were just what you would do or say to anyone you were fond of, that they meant nothing in particular.'

'What things?'

There was a smile hidden somewhere behind that calm face now and she looked hard at him and said decisively, 'I *must* learn to decipher your face or I'll be at a disadvantage forever. I think I can see a smile lurking, but I'm not quite sure. You're so damn good at putting up a façade - it's a bit unnerving.'

'Just tell me, what did I say – or do?'

He's enjoying this and he knows I'm getting embarrassed, she thought, but he's going to tease me about it until I tell him. I can see this kind of game becoming a habit, recurring now and then over the years. And then she felt her face grow hot at how presumptuous but exciting that idea seemed after the last week or two of intermittent misery.

'This is going to sound mad, but the very first time you took hold of my hand, even in the middle of such pain, I felt something – like a current of warmth. And when you kissed my knuckles, the second time we met, that was the first overt thing.'

He smiled and pulled her closer again. 'I did it before I could stop myself, but what I really wanted to do was pull you close and kiss you senseless in front of all those people, but of course, I couldn't – or I thought I couldn't.' After a moment he added seriously, and she could see that he needed her to understand his reasoning, it was important to him. 'And when I thought about that impulse later, I thought I must be very, very careful – a relationship with you wasn't to be – or so I thought - and I had to avoid showing you what I felt, kind of protect you from getting involved.'

'You know what? You're an utter idiot sometimes! We could have avoided all this.' And then she reached up and took his face between her hands and smiled. 'But much against my normal inclinations, I love how you want to look after me, it makes me feel so special. Remember when we went out for drinks, and you told me to stay where I was while you went out to get that tape and stuff? And as you got up, you said, 'Stay here, I mean it - I'm not joking, Sofia!' You sounded quite severe, as if I were a child, and it made me feel safe, protected - I felt as if I belonged to you. I can remember the exact tone of your voice. After you'd gone I sat there with a silly smile on my face thinking about you.'

He chuckled and she leaned against his chest and thought, I love that chuckle and it's even better when

I can feel his chest vibrate – what a gorgeous man he is!

'And I can perfectly remember,' he said, 'how you told me in a voice that made it clear you would tolerate absolutely no nonsense, to sit down on the toilet after you pulled my shorts down. I felt about three years old.'

'You were quite easy to manage once I got the hang of it.' She laughed at the memory. 'And your face! Utter outrage, so funny – if you hadn't been so weak, you would have pulled your shorts up and left. And if I hadn't been so worried, I would have laughed.'

'I don't want to let go of you – not ever really, but I think we should have lunch now. And I know exactly what you were just about to remind me of – I saw that glint of evil mischief, so don't describe it, please. I've had enough embarrassment for one day.'

Sofia stepped back and said innocently, 'Oh, you mean when you could hardly stand upright in the shower, and I had to …?'

He gave her a little shake, and she said, 'But I enjoyed doing it, I really did! I've never had a chance to do that ever before – I could describe it for you, the whole thing, every stroke of my soapy hands and how it felt. I can play it back in my mind any time I like – I know your body so well now.'

'I'm not listening,' he said and walked away towards the kitchen end of the long room. 'How does smoked salmon and poached eggs sound? With toasted ciabatta.'

'You can cook?'

'That's not cooking – that's mostly just putting stuff on a plate, but yes, I can cook. I like cooking.'

'Really? In that case, I'm yours forever,' said Sofia and laughed again. 'How you must have hated the frozen food I dished up - you poor man! Do you think we could have our lunch a bit later, so we can go to bed first?'

Chapter 41

When Sofia got around to telling her mother that she was getting married, Patsy had been back in Auckland for a couple of weeks and spring had morphed into summer. Having eventually worked out why her phone was always on speaker when she called her mother, she decided to turn it to speaker again, so she could introduce Paul, but she soon regretted the decision.

'Really?' said Patsy in a surprised voice. 'Well, it's about time you found someone, I suppose. I hope he's not like that awful man you lived with before, whatever his name was – I didn't like him.'

'Oh no – he's very different, extremely nice, I think you'll like him.' Sofia avoided looking at Paul and kept her gaze on the sea instead. 'Perhaps we should come up for a weekend so you can meet him, or you could come here.'

'I haven't really got time for that right now,' said Patsy briskly. 'We're rehearsing for that concert at the Aotea Centre I told you about —they've added another tenor in the last minute for me to do another duet with, so I need to concentrate on that. But I'm glad you found someone to marry! Sorry, got to rush or I'll be late for a rehearsal, it's with the full orchestra today which is always so exciting. Bye!'

With a sigh Sofia put the phone back on the balcony table and picked up her glass of wine. 'Sorry — I'll introduce you next time I talk to her, or the time after that.'

Paul looked closely at her for a moment and said, 'I don't know how to you put up with it, the dismissive comments, the implied insults. She's very self-absorbed, isn't she, as if she has no time for you and your concerns. But you're so good the way you don't retaliate. I don't know if I would be so tolerant.'

'Good?' Sofia made a face. 'That's got nothing to do with being good, it's just self-preservation. I learned how to do this and avoid trouble from an early age. If I started any kind of argument she might erupt into one her famous tirades about how disappointing I am and how much she's had to put up with. I'll tell her the date later, and we'll see if she has time to come to the wedding.'

He shook his head and put his hand over hers for a moment. He did this often, and every time it made her feel the sensation she first experienced in the café the day she dislocated her finger, and she remembered something else from that day that she should tell him.

'You know the day you rescued me in that café and fixed my finger? And before you started bandaging it up, you put your finger under my chin and made me look straight at you and my eyes were full of tears. You thought it was the pain, but it wasn't. I had just had one of those devastating flashes of insight that you get sometimes when some little detail makes you remember things – or you just understand something. The way you were being so kind and what your touch did to me, made me feel warm and safe – and I realised I hadn't felt like that since I was a tiny child.'

'How is that possible?' he said after a long pause while he studied her face, as if for clues. 'You grew up with your mother after your father died, and you had a long-term relationship with a man who was clearly a controlling bastard, but there must have been love and affection in your life.'

'I think my mother loves me in her own way, but

she was often very impatient and focused on her own concerns – I never felt I could live up to her expectations. Like, when I was little I'd sometimes sit on her knee and she might read me a story or maybe just tell me about something, and then suddenly she'd just push me off her knee and say, "Right, that's enough of that" and go and do something else or pick up her book. Like she had made a motherly gesture and now she was bored.'

She paused again and tried to think how to explain her dysfunctional relationship with Will, the man she had deceived, and realised that she has hardly told Paul anything about it.

'I think I need another glass of wine to explain the next bit.' She smiled. 'I know so much more now, but back then when I was twenty-four or something I was swayed by the desire he felt for me and perhaps lust on my side? I did fall in love with him, but even at the very start I never felt safe. I don't mean physically safe - it was more as if I must constantly try and live up to some idealised version of myself to satisfy him and keep the relationship going. I never felt I could say just anything or dress just anyhow, it was all related to him - how he wanted me to look, how he wanted me to be. And then after a year or so, he said he wanted me to stop taking the pill because he had read something bad about possible long-term effects, and he didn't think it was a good idea. And when I said, what if I get pregnant – thinking of my career - he said we could have a couple of children and then I could have my tubes tied.'

'For Christ's sake! You had to possibly sacrifice your career, you had to have your tubes tied, because something he got into his head? The man was a monster! Helen mentioned he was controlling, but she didn't say in what way.'

'Helen could see it. I mean, she could really see him for what he was, right from the start. He was controlling in many underhand ways, kind of under the radar and I only realised after I left him what it had grown into, and how it had become dangerous for my mental health. I continued taking the pill, I just kept the packet in my desk drawer at work, and on a Friday I'd put two loose pills in the bottom of my bag to cover the weekend. He never found out.'

'And how did you leave him? Did you tell him what you thought about him, or did you just walk out?'

Just thinking about it made her shudder. 'It was awful! Just horrible, far worse than I had imagined it would be. I did try to explain why I couldn't continue in a relationship that had become one of dominance, and his reaction was explosive fury – quite frightening at the time. You know, clenched fists, shouting, coming right up to me when I got to my feet, standing so close he nearly touched me and telling me awful things about my failings. His eyes! Like hatred all of a sudden, as if he couldn't stand the look of me.'

'What did you do? How did you get out of that without being thumped? He sounds dangerous.'

'He stormed out and slammed the door, so I picked up my bag and my briefcase, put my laptop and my chargers into it, chucked my toothbrush and my make-up in, and left. I think I probably closed the door behind my no more than fifteen minutes after he'd gone. I half ran the first bit, only stopped to call a taxi when I was two blocks away – desperate to not stand anywhere near the flat and wait for the taxi in case he came back and spotted me. I spent the night with Helen and Oscar, who had just moved in with her, and the next day I rang in sick, and Helen took the day off and we drove to the flat in her car – I didn't have one then. We waited outside until he'd gone to work and then we went in and cleared out every single thing that was mine, just threw things in bags and carried clothes draped over our arms down to the car and drove away. I've only exchanged a couple of sentences with him since, when he became a nuisance.'

The look on Paul's face was hard to interpret,

and Sofia said quietly, 'What are you thinking. I can't decode your face.'

'I'm furious on your behalf, and at the same time I feel sorry for what he did to you, and I also admire how you didn't cave in. Because that kind of man would probably return after a couple of hours and tell you how much he loved you and ask you to forgive him and promise never to be so angry again - or something along those lines. But you just left - brilliant move! Did he try to contact you?'

'Oh yes - in the end, I had to get a new phone number, he flooded me with messages, alternating abuse with promising how he would improve, and apologies. Classic for his type of man, as you said. But though he must have guessed where I was, he never turned up at Helen's – he wouldn't have dared. I think he knew she'd report him for harassment or stalking or something. Once he tried to waylay me outside where I worked then, but I told him to go away, or I would scream for help and people would stop and he left.'

Very late that evening, Sofia looked at Paul in the dim light filtering in through the bedroom window and said, 'You know what? We are *so* good at sex! Stupendously good.'

'Meant to be together. Are you happy? I feel so different, it's like a miracle.'

'Very different,' she said and put her hand on his cheek. 'As carefree and happy as anyone could be, nothing can weigh me down now – I feel lighter than air.'

They spent nearly the whole Saturday moving the last things from Sofia's apartment after a week of sorting and making decisions, taking boxes down in the lift and trying to be rational about how much kitchen equipment and how many coffee mugs they could possibly need.

'We shouldn't have left it to the last minute,' Sofia said at breakfast on Sunday morning. 'It's not as if we didn't know the new owner takes over next Friday. I'll go over there straight from work tomorrow and load up all the stuff to go to the op-shop and then I can clean the place on Tuesday or Wednesday night, and then it's all done.'

'We'll do it together – it won't take long, it's easy to clean when the place is empty. I did it in my old house when I moved here, and it was surprisingly quick once all the obstacles were removed. So, are you going to stop prevaricating and call your mother? I'd like to talk to her, if she's not in a rush.'

'Really? You've heard how difficult she can be – and you want to talk to her?'

'I would like to start my relationship with her on my own terms, instead of spending the rest of my life flinching every time she hurts you. I'm not going to be rude, but I'd like to draw a line in the sand before I meet her face to face. A demarcation line if you like - and provided you don't mind, of course. She might decide she can't stand me, but I don't think I can put up with hearing you being treated like this. What do you think? Is it taking too big a risk? Will she take it out on you?'

'What would you say to her?'

'I'm not sure – enough to make her understand that I've got your back whatever she says in future, that I'm not putting up with it. I just think it's time someone stood between her and you and stopped this evil habit of belittling you for no reason. It's not acceptable.'

Sofia continued to unload the dishwasher while she thought about it and ended up standing with a last coffee mug in her hand and a faraway look on her face for so long without moving that Paul took a step closer.

'You're not about to drop that, are you?' He took the mug out of her hand and put it away, then closed the dishwasher and left her alone in the kitchen. She hardly noticed because in her mind she was weighing up the potential fall-out from the demarcation line suggestion and also projecting a future where her mother would never again make her feel alternatingly mildly unsatisfactory and downright devoid of good qualities. A future where there would be someone beside her to step in and put a stop to the denigrating comments. She gave herself a little shake, picked up her phone from the kitchen bench and went to sit opposite Paul, who was in his favourite armchair with a book.

'OK, feel free to do your knight in shining armour thing – I don't really care what you say, I'll just be grateful for the protection and the support.'

'Hi, mum,' said Sofia a few minutes later, having caught her mother just after she had returned home from a meeting. 'How did the concert go? I read some good reviews.'

'It went well – better than well actually when you consider some of the issues we had. One tenor down with a stomach bug, a replacement whose voice was a shade too dark to sing a duet with a mezzo, and someone in the dress circle whose phone went off twice!'

'We're getting married on the twenty-fourth of December, when a lot of Paul's relatives are in town. Will you be able to come?'

'Oh, I think so. Unless something pops up in the meantime. I thought I might go down and visit Fliss in January some time, I haven't seen her for ages. Now, tell me, who is this Paul person? What does he do?'

As Sofia hesitated, Paul reached for the phone. 'Hi Patsy, it's Paul. I might as well introduce myself. I 'm a Crown prosecutor – I work mainly in Wellington.'

There was an unusual moment of silence at the other end, while Patsy presumably digested this. 'I thought you were the chap who helped Sofia when she hurt her finger,' she said finally. 'Was that somebody else?'

'No, that was me – I was a paramedic with St John's before I studied law.'

Another silence and Sofia held her breath, because these silences were so unusual, very different from Patsy's normal way of firing off comments and questions.

'So, you *are* the man in that photo on social media, the one someone took through the café window?'

'Yes, I am.'

'Well, that's encouraging, I suppose – she's not the best at forming relationships, so let's hope it's going to work out this time. I presume you think it will, seeing you're marrying her.'

'Listen, Patsy, I think we'd better get a couple of things clear from the start, just so we know where we stand.' Now his voice was the one he sometimes used in court, Sofia recognised it and wondered how this was going to pan out. Either very well or utter disaster, she thought, and sat as if frozen, her eyes on her hands clenched on her lap. Any moment now her mother might either launch an attack or just put the phone done.

'Here's how it looks from my end,' continued Paul. 'Sofia gets very little recognition, if any, from you. I've listened to a few of your conversations now, and I don't like what I hear. I also know she's always trying to keep things on an even keel with you, so she never protests, never stands up for herself. And I don't like that either, so here are a few things we need to get straight. For a start, Sofia is a great communicator and has a large circle of friends who all love her. Her extended family adore her. She is a fantastic barrister, and shines in the courtroom, clear, calm and concise. She has an amazing memory, huge rafts of detailed facts at her fingertips, hardly ever refers to her notes and displays compassion in all she does. I wouldn't be at all surprised if she becomes the youngest King's Counsel in the country one day. She is also funny, sexy and kind. As far as I can see, her only failing is that she can't cook, which doesn't matter, because I can. And here's another thing – I'm not marrying her, we're marrying each other.'

Sofia couldn't lift her eyes to Paul's face, her cheeks were burning, and her heart was beating faster than normal as she waited for the outburst which was now sure to come. But instead of a tirade or the call being ended abruptly, after a long pause Patsy said appreciatively, 'Amazing man! *Fabulous* delivery! You are something else again, as they say. I hope you'll be very happy together – and I'll try to be a bit … softer, I suppose.'

Paul said goodbye, put the phone on the table and Sofia burst out laughing. 'Perfect!' she said. 'I can't believe you got away with that. And even if you exaggerated quite a bit, it worked – she didn't challenge a single thing you said. Must have been your fabulous delivery!'

He got up, bent to kiss the top of her head and chuckled. 'Maybe she responds well to domineering men, even if it was an act? But, seriously, I think it went well, and when we meet I'll make sure she knows that line in the sand is permanent.'

Chapter 43

When the invitations went out for the Christmas Eve party with drinks and a buffet dinner, the reason given was "to thank everyone for their hospitality during the past year" and the fact that only a small portion of them had offered either Sofia or Paul hospitality was beside the point. Most people took it to mean that this was just their way of getting everyone together; a newly formed couple celebrating their first Christmas together.

'Lots of them won't come,' said Sofia a few days before Christmas. 'They'll be on their way to Honolulu or to their parents' place in Timbuktu or whatever. I wish people weren't so hopeless about replying to invitations. It's as if they don't know what RSVP means. Maybe we should have made it

278

a week before Christmas rather than the day before.'

'I sincerely hope most of them come,' said Paul and held up the quote from the caterers he had just printed out. 'We're catering for fifty-six people, and it's impossible to predict how many might not come, I mean, a family group could remove half a dozen in one go. But we're getting supplies for that number, so if half of them don't come we'll just have to give the rest to the City Mission for their charity Christmas dinner.'

At eleven o'clock in the morning on Christmas Eve, Sofia and Paul were married in the Botanical gardens with only four guests present.

'It's like a secret wedding,' said Ursula when she hugged Sofia after the minimal ceremony. 'I love the way you can get married outdoors in parks and things, and this is such a lovely setting. And I must say your vows were very touching but just a tiny bit mysterious. I do hope you will explain exactly what the meaning is at some later date.

'We might,' said Sofia and tried not to laugh. 'It depends on how comfortable Paul is with letting some personal emotional stuff out of the bag, so to speak.'

'Only tell us if you feel like it,' said Helen and shot a mischievous look at Sofia. 'We wouldn't want you to reveal anything deeply personal and intimate. I can imagine Paul prefers to keep some things to himself.'

'Oh, it's just something we thought was significant and worth including via a brief reference. When the celebrant asked us to write our own vows, we didn't know where to start. It's not as easy as it sounds, and those she gave as examples just didn't fit the bill for us.'

She glanced at Paul, whose conversation with Patsy and Oscar a few steps away seemed to be interlaced with a surprising amount of laughter.

Helen followed her look and smiled. 'Your mum's taken to Paul in a big way. It's a bit rude to point it out, but I've never seen her engage with anyone in such relaxed way.'

'No, not even with me,' said Sofia and choked back a laugh. 'She loves him, thinks he's amazing for some reason.'

I wish I had recorded that phone call, thought Sofia, then I could play it back to Helen, because she deserves to know about it. Without her we might never have sorted ourselves out.

There was no way she could tell Helen here and now what had brought about this transformation in

Patsy, but at some time in the future she would; the story of Paul drawing his line in the sand over the phone with Patsy was simply too good not to share.

'Lunch at Oriental Bay,' said Paul a few moments later. 'An early lunch so we can get back to the house and get organised before the caterers arrive at five – we've got a lot of furniture to move. The taxi van should be at the end of this path in five minutes, I ordered it for half past eleven.'

The Boat Café was the perfect place on a sunny summer day. Their table on the balcony was right beside the railing, the sunshine glittered on the waves, and seagulls screeched overhead. When they their champagne had been poured and they had ordered, Helen rose to her feet and tapped her glass.

'This is a special day for me,' she said. 'I have witnessed my very special best friend getting married to an amazing guy and I know they will be happy. Their love story, which I have played a small part in, is probably the best one I've ever heard of. Instant love at first sight, heart-breaking misunderstandings and an ending fit for a storybook. Here's to Sofia and Paul!'

Everyone clapped, people at the next table, who had stopped talking to listen, joined in and Patsy said, 'Hear, hear!'

Paul put his hand over Sofia's on the table and

said, 'I know there were parts of the wedding vows you wondered about, and this is the time to explain. I'm keeping this lowkey and I'm not standing up, because I don't want everyone at the tables around us to listen in. I haven't checked with my wife – first time I've said that! – but if I go too far she'll stop me, she knows how to do it. So, this is what the strange sentence in our vows was about. When we were on our first date I fell ill with a severe bout of flu that hit me, as Sofia puts it, like a tidal wave – high temperature, delirium, sick as a dog.'

He looked at Sofia and smiled. 'And she dragged me to her place which luckily wasn't far away and looked after me for four days, large parts of which I can't remember at all. Wiping me down with wet cloths, changing the sheets, sitting up all night – several nights – watching over me and forcing me, despite my confused efforts to resist, to drink copious amounts of water. And then we got to the stage when we both needed a shower after several days and nights of fever and perspiration. I because I was sick and Sofia because she hadn't taken the time to look after herself. She supported me to the shower, stripped my boxers off and turned the water on – and thankfully she kept watching because my knees buckled, and I started sliding down the wall, unable to stand up. And what did she do?'

He smiled at Sofia again, and continued, ignored her imploring look. 'She stripped her clothes off in record time and got in with me, told me to lean against the wall and proceeded to wash me from top to toe – no parts neglected – with lovely soapy hands, which even in my befuddled and exhausted state I enjoyed. And now we go back to how it started. I saw her dislocate her finger in that famous café, as you all know, and attended to her on the spot, and much later she told me how she had felt a current of warmth when I touched her, and how she wished I wouldn't let go of her hand. So, the phrase "with the benefit and blessing of our four hands" refers to private moments - which I would prefer you don't write about on social media.'

Chapter 44

After a prolonged lunch, which had started early but turned into a very long lunch, Paul pushed his chair back and got to his feet.

'We'll see you tonight at six,' he said. 'We've just got to get back, change our clothes and finish moving stuff in the living room. Yesterday afternoon, which was when we had planned to do it, we ended up with a hoard of visitors just popping in as they called it – my two sisters, their husbands and children, one dog and one hanger-on. And they stayed for hours, we had pizza delivered for dinner and all the stuff we had planned to do didn't get done.'

Sofia laughed and shook her head at how disorganised they were after various ad hoc visits. 'And that was only Paul's side of the family. Yesterday morning my aunt Fliss accompanied by her son and daughter and two grandchildren texted at ten and said they were brining morning tea and wanted to meet Paul before the party tonight. So that took a good couple of hours. Paul's sisters and company arrived at three which took up the next five hours, and when *they* left and we had tidied up, we fell into bed exhausted. So, nothing much got done as planned.'

To Sofia's surprise Patsy did not go off to meet someone in town or "do something" but got into Paul's car with them and returned to the house.

'Oh no, of course not,' she said. 'What do you take me for? There's work to be done and it will be quicker with three of us than just you two.'

Sofia smiled inwardly at this additional benefit of what she privately referred to as "the son-in-law love affair". No way would her mother have offered to shift furniture around and help set up for a large party before she fell for Paul. Unexpected benefits, she thought, as surprising as the nearly constant good mood she's in these days. I wonder if she's on medication or if it's just a complete change of personality. Or maybe I've finally lived up to her expectations, found a man she can accept and now she's prepared to overlook my other shortcomings.

. . .

By half past six the house was packed, the large folding doors were open to extend the living room out to the big balcony that ran along the full width of the house, and excess furniture had been put away in the bedrooms. The caterers had set up their stainless-steel trolleys on the bottom floor and had commandeered the kitchen, and wait staff were in place.

'Do we really need all these people?' Sofia had said when the arrangements were made with the caterers. 'A barman and three wait staff as well as those dealing with the food?'

'Let's do it properly and then we can enjoy ourselves without having to worry about things,' Paul had said. 'We're only doing this once – I hope – so let's do it in style.'

Now Sofia put her glass down on the kitchen counter and went to rescue Margot's husband Phil from the triplets who had decided that his trick of making coins disappear and reappear by magic must mean there was more to come.

'Hey, you lot!' she said when she reached them. 'I'll tell you a secret – this is the only trick he knows - his wife told me. But my new nieces and nephews have brought four big boxes of construction sets and whatever, and they're just getting things out in the study now, so why don't you go and inspect what they're doing.'

The triplets disappeared and Phil laughed. 'I think one of those rascals kept my two-dollar coin, but never mind. I'll go and get another glass of wine while I can. And whose is that serious little thing following Paul around wherever he goes? The Asiatic looking one.'

'My former neighbour's little girl, Bitsy. She's in love with him too.' She grinned. 'She told me last weekend when she came to stay the night that when Paul gets tired of me she's going to marry him.'

In a room so full of voices it was extraordinary to be able to hear just one sentence, separated from rest, thought Sofia, when she heard Helen say, 'I love this view, I could stand here forever and look out over the sea.'

Sofia sidled behind Barton and Margot and one of Paul's brothers-in-law and joined Helen who was talking to Ursula and Clare on the balcony.

'Thank God the weather is so good, or we'd have been squashed up in the living room,' she said. 'This balcony is a life saver – like having another room. I love being out here, it's a bit like being in the prow of a boat – you're high above the ground and the water seems so close.'

Ursula smiled. 'When Paul sent me a link to this house on some real estate company's website – this was before I moved back from Denmark – I thought it was an amazing house, and then he said he wasn't buying it after all, because he didn't need a three-bedroom house with a separate study and a double garage. So, though I agreed he didn't need such a big house, I replied and said, please buy it, you're just the kind of guy who will happily sit just gazing at the horizon instead of reading the book in your hand, and if you feel lonely I'll come and share the house with you. But now he doesn't feel lonely at all and I've found a nice little flat right in the middle of town, which is just what I like.'

'That's exactly what he does – he sits in his favourite chair just inside the glass wall and half the time he's not even reading, he's just looking out and thinking,' said Sofia, and then she realised that this was the first time these two women had met, and it made her smile. 'I don't know what you two have discovered already, but you both play a major role in this story. Ursula, has Helen told you about the crucial role she played in how all this came about? If she hadn't intervened this wedding would never have happened.'

'Oh, do tell me, please,' said Ursula and Sofia left them to it and went to find her husband.

Many Thanks

We hope you've enjoyed reading this story and would consider leaving a review on your favourite review site, or with the retailer you purchased from.

These are not only much appreciated, they also help other readers discover new authors.

For more in this ongoing series, plus other titles, please read on.

Letters from the Past

Letters from the Past is a series of stand-alone novels where a letter from or about the past reveals something that changes a woman's perceptions of herself or of her family, and that affects her outlook on life.

These books are such fun to write, and I am always working on the next title in this series. I hope you will enjoy reading them as much as I enjoy writing them!

Tina

Having had nobody in her life since her husband died, Lara unexpectedly finds herself involved with three men. One is planning to use her, one she plans to use for her own ends, and one becomes a "friend-with-benefits" with surprising results. Sometimes a quiet schoolteacher is not all she seems at first glance.

Callista experiences an event of apparent ESP at the Okehampton Castle ruins and becomes a media sensation, but the effect it has on her life is dramatic. How do two people, one calm. one seriously claustrophobic, who feel they are poles apart, cope for an hour and a half in total darkness in a stalled lift? And can they handle the consequences?

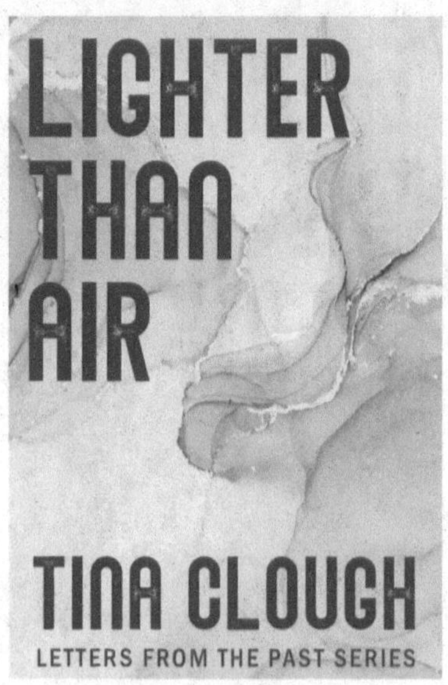

Sofia's life is in turmoil: a difficult diva mother, a letter with a confession about a family killing and having to accept help from a man she loathes when she is injured. Can reluctant attraction turn into love?

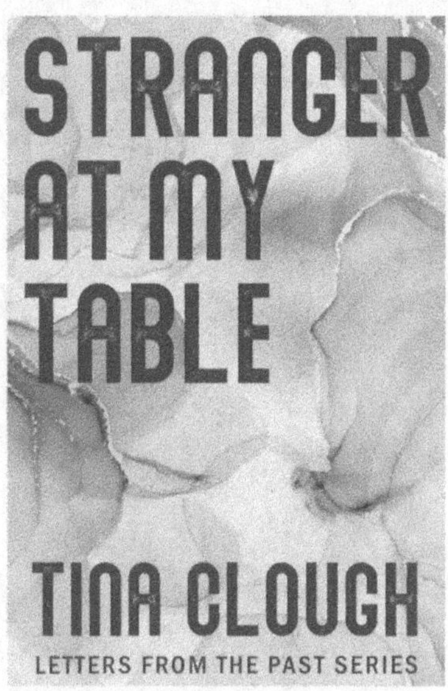

Who is the stranger living in the empty house Miranda inherited from her grandmother? Why is he living like a secretive recluse in someone else's house? Reckless Miranda decides to confront him, and what she discovers prompts her to set out on a fearless quest to bring justice to a man who has given up hope. But is the gamble too great or a risk worth taking?

When Emma finds an old letter in a library book she is instantly intrigued, but by researching the origin of the letter she unwittingly opens the door to danger and becomes the target for threats and harassment. Nearly desperate, she takes a leap of blind faith into the unknown and accepts an offer of help from a stranger - but can she trust him?

Jamie, an ardent protester against the gigantic Vista Resort development and Leo Masters, the high-powered developer, seem unlikely to ever agree on anything. But unexpected coincidences and chance brings them together in a fragile state of mutual respect. Will courage and kindness resolve the situation, or do they need help?

After a bizarre accident with ESP overtones, the media haunt Arapera. But can she trust an offer of help from a man she has only met once? Or will she regret it for the rest of her life if she doesn't take the chance? Sometimes life is a knife-edge balance between staying safe and taking risks, and there is no way of predicting if the gamble is worth it.

Also by Tina Clough

THE GIRL WHO LIVED TWICE

What would you do if you woke up one morning and found that time had rewound exactly a year? Would you revisit your past mistakes and try to do better? Would you try to get revenge on those who had wronged you? Or would you use what you knew to get rich? When Mia finds herself in her own past, she must decide how best to use her pre-knowledge of one year's worth of events and personal issues.

RUNNING TOWARDS DANGER

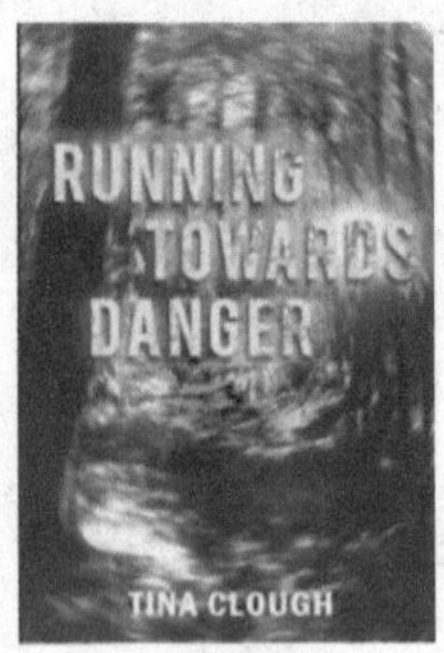

When Karen's flat-mate Nick is gunned down in front of her in the street her life is turned upside-down. Everything she thought she knew about him turns out to be a lie. She becomes a suspect in the police investigation and drug bosses think she knows where Nick has hidden a large sum of money. When her life is threatened, she decides to leave town and disappear.

Karen becomes Cara and creates an anonymous existence, severs all links to her past and adopts a cash-based way of life that leaves no electronic traces. But despite her careful planning danger still stalks her and she is forced to make dramatic choices in the face of threats and brutal violence.

Can she trust the man she is attracted to, or has he been sent by the killers to gain her confidence and find the money they believe she has?

THE CHINESE PROVERB

Book 1 - Hunter Grant Series

Army veteran Hunter Grant thought he had left war behind in Afghanistan – a conflict that left him with physical and psychological scars.

But finding an unconscious girl in the Northland bush and gradually untangling her story involves him in warfare of a different kind in his own country.

Hunter sets out to find and punish the man Dao calls Master, but he soon finds there is more to this story than enslavement. Before long he himself is being hunted by the overlord of a drug empire whose sole objective is to kill Dao because she knows too much.

Protecting her and waging war while trying to keep the police from stifling his enterprise takes all Hunter's ingenuity and determination and puts him in deadly jeopardy.

ONE SINGLE THING

Book 2 - Hunter Grant Series

Journalist Hope Barber disappears two weeks after returning to New Zealand from an assignment in Pakistan, leaving her front door open and her bag and phone inside. The police are tight-lipped about their reluctance to act, and Hunter Grant and Dao agree to help Hope's brother Noah find her. Details about Hope's time in Pakistan gradually emerge but only raise more questions.

Was Hope under surveillance?

Was she linked to terrorists?

And who is the man Hope called 'my stalker'?

FOLDED

Book 3 - Hunter Grant Series

First notes asking for help and folded into tiny origami shapes are found outside a city apartment building, then a physics textbook with tiny writing between the lines and then the woman who found them abruptly resigns and disappears. Are the notes asking for help real or is it a game? Hunter Grant, ex-army and with a pragmatic view of justice, reluctantly agrees to help find the missing woman.

Things get complicated when a high-powered lawyer arrives form the US, and shortly after his meeting with Hunter and Dao, a "cease and desist" letter arrives from the Cayman Islands. Inspector Bakker - a woman, who in Hunter's words "looks as if she would be useful in a brawl, provided she was on your side" - takes instant exception to his involvement and threatens to arrest him for interfering in an investigation.

Dao sets out alone on a dangerous mission, driven by a compulsive need to find out what has happened to the girl who wrote the notes, and Hunter looks death in the face when he decides to risk everything to put an end to the Darknet forces that threaten their lives.

THE SHADOW BROKER

It is 2026 and individual freedoms are severely curtailed, with state surveillance everywhere. State Security has a Watch List, and being on it means that nothing you do or say escapes the authorities, but does the Kill List really exist? And if it does, how would you know if you were on it?

Coded messages on a found burner phone, top-level government corruption and a shadowy mastermind who calls himself The Broker. In this climate of state control, three unlikely friends start quietly looking for connections and set in motion a deadly game of hide and seek that will change their lives forever.

Trying to uncover the truth means risking your life, and nothing is more dangerous than searching for evidence of government corruption.

About the Author

Tina Clough grew up in Sweden and now lives in New Zealand; dividing her time between writing fiction and translating and editing medical research papers.

Between working and writing she looks after an acre of fruit trees, vegetable gardens and roaming hens.

Apart from reading her interests include photography, wine, growing organic vegetables, making jam and kayaking.

https://lightpoolpublishing.com

9 781991 187147